This is a love letter to you, Midwesterners. And a taste of what we're made of, for those on the outside looking in. We see you, and we're glad you're here.

About the Cover Artist

Katie Stapleton is a lifelong resident of the Toledo area, married for 16 years to her husband Matt. She is an amateur photographer, fan of local history, genealogy, antiques, and spontaneous road trips. She and her husband currently reside in Oregon, Ohio.

Our cover image, a photograph titled "Waiting for Tome (The Toledo Train Station)," was captured while visiting the station, in April 2022. Her and her husband Matt were scoping the set of where the next big Hollywood movie would take place (*A Man Called Otto*, featuring Tom Hanks). As they planned their next adventure, she stopped and became inspired on how the sun glistened and captured the moment of the past, present, and future of the Toledo Rails. The past can tell stories, the present still gives purpose, and the future are the stories looking down the rails yet to be told.

Made of Rust and Glass

Volume II

Made of Rust and Glass, Volume II

Edited by Curtis A. Deeter, Leah McNaughton Lederman, and Jonie McIntire

Published by:
Of Rust and Glass
607 River Road
Maumee, OH 43537

Typesetting: Curtis A. Deeter

Cover Art: Katie Stapleton

ISBN: 978-1-7367728-9-8

A Good Start

by Susan Coultrap-McQuin

Susan Coultrap-McQuin is a retired educator, avid gardener, and world traveler. Her chapbook of travel poems, What We Bring Home, *(The Poetry Box) was released in 2021. Other recent poems have appeared in* Still Point Arts Quarterly, The Dewdrop, Lowestoft Chronicle, Quiet Diamonds, Talking Stick, The Moccasin, The Poeming Pidgeon, *and several pandemic-themed anthologies. A supporter of public art, Susan has also displayed poems in art galleries, libraries, and parks, and she helps organize readings for the arts consortium in her Minnesota county. She has earned several awards for her poems, including being a finalist in the Orchard Street Poetry Contest and an honorable mention from Wick Poetry Center.*

He'd shake us early, the cabin still dark, floor cold under our feet. Half asleep, my sister and I pulled sweaters over heads, said not a word. We grabbed our poles, Dad, the tackle box, and out we fast-walked to the dock with its hollow moans, swaying side to side. We climbed in a wooden boat, rented by the week, grabbed a seat. Dad's hand shoved the boat from its berth.

We'd drift a bit, look back to silence on shore, before he pulled the cord. On days the motor wouldn't start, he swore. When it sputtered to life, we'd chug away, watch the bubbled "V" of our wake. "Which way, girls?" We'd point or shrug and off we'd go to a distant spot, no other boats, only loons in pairs, slipping under water as we passed. Dad liked to chase them, but not at this hour.

We'd anchor near a promising spot, the right weeds, the right drop. The morning fog hung like tips of a veil over slate gray waters. Into shadows we threw three red and white bobbers, sat perfectly still. My thoughts drifted to bears and wolves on the darker shore, the story I'd write of escape. I'd wait and wait and wait, until I felt a gentle tug, looked to see my bobber bob, first one wave circling, then three, then five.

"Give it a quick jerk, set the hook," Dad whispered, grabbed the net. He'd coach me until the bobber dipped, fully wet, pulled away, disappeared. It might be a sunfish, a bluegill, or, lucky day, a hungry walleye we'd eat at noon. The hardest fight was the most fun. But any fish in the net got a "Well done."

Too soon Dad would say, "It's breakfast time. What do you suppose Mom fixed?" With a stringer of fish, we were ready. We pulled in our poles, sat steady on our seats. And, at that moment, I remember the sun rose, the shore turned mossy green, the lake glittered blue, and loons began to sing.

Two Poems
by Robert Beveridge

Robert Beveridge (he/him) makes noise and writes poetry in Akron, OH. Recent/upcoming appearances in Medium Chill, Cold Moon Journal, *and* The Parliament Journal, *among others. (xterminal.bandcamp.com)*

Into the Alley

Whisper of rain on asphalt
still warm from faded day.
Your path lies between an adult
cinema and a diner known
for its key lime pie. Reflected
streetlamp glow fades after
just a few steps. Obstacles
are shadow.

       Crouch behind
a dumpster and listen. You
hear rain. Slip off your shoes.
Quiet travel. Your shirt wet
against your skin, heavier
than darkness. Too much
to carry. A few more steps
and you stand against
the back wall, alone.

Behind you lights
and car horns attempt
penetration, fail.
Sound of a police whistle.
You stand, shirtless, wet,
a hint of citrus in your nose.
Hands and back
against the wall. It surprises you
with its softness. It has the feel
of the day, the moistness
of long rain. You would pull it

about you like a blanket
if you could.
                Above you
the stars. Look up, clutch one
hand tight in the other. This
is where you are and it
has always been right.

Wheel of Fortune (reversed)

As if sunset were a wall, compression
a hammer. As if the ice had never
made it to the tray in the first place.
As if thirty-seven trillion (who may
or may not be Elvis fans) could never
be wrong, but also as if the census taker
could not, indeed, count that high
in the first place. As if "calf" and "bonfire"
were interchangeable in the same way
as "alcohol" and "fish tank." As if
the jackbooted thugs had moved
into the neighborhood and the resistance
pushed them back as far as, say,
Winnetka before they all stopped
exercises to wait for the ground to thaw.
As if at any moment a rogue messenger
might break the shield wall with a scroll
signed in salt, bound in sand, and sprint
with all his might to Marathon, thus
bringing the world to an end.

But it hasn't happened yet.

Last Trip to Drive Sol

(first appeared in *Of Rust and Glass's* "Summer")

by Bobbi Rae

Bobbi Rae is a reclusive author of literary and romantic fiction. Their work is often reflective of real-life events and focuses on shared experiences and emotions.

If you asked us where Drive Sol was, we wouldn't have been able to say. Somewhere between afternoon bike rides, making out with girls on the bench behind Sunoco, and romps in the backseat of Evan's Buick. We'd be quick to say it didn't really matter.

Our first trip to Drive Sol was against a rising summer sun, Red Hot Chilli Peppers echoing across the soy fields. We were dreaming of Ohiofornication. We were Hollywood, living our teenage years trapped in a fantasy of super stardom and wasted youth, convinced that we were it, and nobody was going to tell us any different.

We called it our "brown route." It was straight roads and potholes, crooked barns and quarries. All said, the route took us an hour through Southeast Michigan and Northwest Ohio. Two, if we pulled over to take a leak or shoot the breeze over a Natty tall boy. Our brown route was for sticking our heads out the window and screaming our angst at sixty miles an hour and putting our little suburban prison as far behind us as we could. It was for smoking middies and getting high off inconsequential middle-class rebellions.

If you asked us why Drive Sol, we wouldn't have had the slightest clue, but we found ourselves back there three times that summer. It was a calling, a pull of gravity we were too weak to resist.

That first trip, it was just three of us. We pulled off the road, into the overgrown parking lot, and sat at the edge of the grass, swatting mosquitos as we watched the afternoon pass us by. From what we could tell, it was just another abandoned manufacturing dump, another business forgotten in a post-industrial age, an oasis kitty-corner to a place where everyone knew your name.

We pieced cigarettes and told stories, listened to the distant whisper of traffic from Route 20, and sat closer than we'd have liked to admit. Friendship at that age was superficial, fleeting. Except at Drive Sol. At Drive Sol, everything lasted forever.

As the sun set, the sky faded to a deep, dark purple, speckled with stars who shared the small secrets of the universe. They were mirrored by a thousand fireflies, where we were no longer sure which way was up and which way was down.

We left Drive Sol when we ran out of Kools and nobody had anything left to say. We left knowing we'd be back, sooner rather than later.

Our second trip, we came in a fleet of Daddy's convertibles and junkyard picks with a case of Natty Light, a fifth of Bacardi, mixtapes burned off LimeWire, and a longing to dance the night away. We kept Evan's car running until its battery died, bumpin' Bone Thugs-n-Harmony and TI, singing along to The Offspring and Reel Big Fish loud enough for the cows to hear. We started a fire near Drive Sol's back bays. Someone brought firewood, and we all brought fire.

It was Friday night, and we stayed until the sun came up, laughing, drinking, smoking, screwing. We stayed until the last drop, then we went our separate ways, dispersing into morning like startled starlings, flying away to find our own proverbial worms, whatever those might be.

Our third trip ended in flashing red and blue. For most of us, it was only the beginning.

We were young. We were stupid. We were blind to obvious signs: the farmhouse across the street, the chickens stirring in their coop, the suspicious parting of miniblinds. Drive Sol itself was not as abandoned as we'd thought. People worked there and surely wondered what the hell was going on in their parking lot after they punched out for the weekend, but we didn't notice the security cameras they had installed.

Most of all, we were blind to the fact that we were not infallible.

We showed up in the Buick, just the three of us, ready for another consequence-free good time. Evan had just bought an AK from the firearms shop across the tracks. We had walked there after school. None of us had ever shot a gun before, but we were bulletproof. So, we loaded it up and fired off round after round into the fields surrounding Drive Sol.

We never found out what happened to that gun, but we know what happened to Evan. We were lucky, in a sense. He was the only one of us plucked from youth that day.

That's the funny thing about growing up, isn't it? Most of us come out on the other side, battered and bruised but more or less better off for our mistakes. But some of us? Well, some of us get stuck in that one summer, no matter how much time passes or how much distance we put between ourselves and the people we leave behind.

Some of us never leave Drive Sol, but if you ask us why, we won't be able to say.

Abuela Butterfly
by Christina C. Moore

Christina Moore lives in Columbus, Ohio. By day, she works as a cataloger in the libraries at The Ohio State University. By night, she writes mysteries and speculative fiction—either science fiction or horror, depending on her mood. She enjoys cycling, photography, aquarium fish, choral music, big dogs, and rogue house cats. She has two other upcoming short story publications, one with the Ohio Writer's Association, the other on the World's Within fantasy blog.

Flowers stream past in a river of pinks, reds, and yellows. I'd like to stop--to grasp their soft petals between my fingers, but the pace of the stroller is relentless. The best I can manage is to brush a large broad leaf with a single outstretched fingertip.

When Abuela takes me to visit the flowers, I always wear shorts with a T-shirt. Since Mommy is taking me, this is a special occasion, and I must be nicely dressed. My dress has two rows of ruffles under the skirt and was a present from my other Grandma who lives far away. I know her through boxes tied with bright ribbon. She knows me through the paintings I make with Abuela and mail in large cardboard envelopes. Other Grandma says that the dress makes me look like her favorite flower, the daffodil. She tells me that I am her daffodil, her favorite flower.

Because I have the kind of hair that will not curl, Mommy pulled it into two tight braids done up with bows. The braids are sore against my scalp and my shoes pinch, but I look like a princess, and looking like a princess makes Mommy happy. "Beauty is pain," she tells me whenever she brushes my hair.

I will wear this outfit next week at Easter, when the church is filled with yellow and white lilies, or so Abuela says. I remember this day from last year because the priest brought a lamb into the church, and I got to touch its soft wool. I was unable to touch the flowers though. They were all high up near the altar where I am not allowed to go.

Mommy is on her phone, her heels clicking across hard tile as she races us forward. The further we head into the emerald greenhouse jungle, the louder her voice becomes. She never notices when other people are staring. "It's the wrong shade," she scolds into the phone. "The foyer needs to be blush. Your guys painted it pink…I don't care what was on the can, the paint was mixed incorrectly and looks terrible."

"Pink!" I exclaim, pointing towards a cluster of fast-approaching flowers. My room is pink. The cover on my big girl's bed is pink too, with embroidered roses. Abuela and I picked it out together on the computer. My other Grandma sent me a pink lamp to match with a shade that looks like a tulip drooping in the rain.

"Just a minute," Mommy barks into the phone. "Harper, honey, you need to be quiet, Mommy is doing business."

"Pink!" I shout again, louder this time. Maybe if I keep yelling the word pink, people will glare at me instead of at her.

"Look, I have to go," Mommy says. "My kid's acting up, but you'd better make this right by the time my clients get back from Tahoe…I don't care if you have other jobs. You're being paid to do this one right."

She drops the phone into her handbag, and we abruptly veer off the main path into the little alcove where there is a fishpond. The fish are long, golden, and brightly speckled as if God has flicked them with paint.

Whenever they spot people, they swarm to the edge of the pond in a frenzy, popping to the surface, mouths open, fins spinning in expectation. At first, I think Mommy is going to put a quarter in the food dispenser so we can feed them. This is what Abuela does, calling them by silly names as she drops a pellet into each gaping mouth. Instead, Mommy looks down at me, and I tilt my head painfully upwards so I can gaze into her clear blue eyes.

The light shining down gives her a halo, and for a second, she looks like a golden angel, like the ones that fly across the ceiling of the big church where we go on Sundays. Mommy and I do not match. She is sunshine against blue sky, while I am dark and moon-faced like Daddy and Abuela. I am Mommy's little princess, but I am also her changeling.

We are alone in this little corner of the greenhouse, surrounded by the clean smells of growing plants and running water. I feel a rush of happiness to be with her in this special place. She smiles down, her lips stretch wide across her narrow face. It's when I notice the hardness in her eyes that I realize she has not rolled me here to feed the fish. Yanking one of my braids, she snaps, "This is your first warning." Even after she lets go, my scalp throbs. Everything about Mommy is beautiful except for her voice.

Suddenly, we are moving again, out through the greenhouse and down a long hallway covered with photographs of oversized flowers in thick black frames. I want to cry, but I don't want my second warning, and so I remain silent, stifling tears in Teddy's soft head.

A lady with silver hair smiles as we race by. She holds a long brown bug rimmed with countless legs. The bug is as big as her hands, which she keeps moving to prevent it from scurrying away. Her smile makes her eyes twinkle. I want to meet this old woman with her friendly smile and strange creature, but Mommy swerves to the other side of the hall. She cannot see the woman, but she certainly sees the bug.

The end of the hallway is covered with glass, an entry way to another world. This greenhouse is big and new, the large door flanked by towering palms. A line of people trails halfway down the hall. Their voices blend, intermingling with the sound of falling water. Abuela told me something special was being built here, and I would have to wait until it is open to explore inside. Now that the time has finally come, I am excited, but also sad that she is not the one here with me. This thought fills me with shame because Mommy is taking her entire day and spending it only on me.

A man with a shaggy beard sits on a tall stool by the door. He won't let us through until all the people lined up ahead of us have gotten their turn.

"See what you've done?" Mommy hisses into my ear. "We have to wait longer because you were so bad." I wonder if I'm about to get my second warning, but instead she takes the phone out of her handbag, and fingernails the color of lady bugs race across its flickering screen.

I don't mind waiting in this line because both walls are covered with huge photographs, each of a different butterfly on a different flower.

Abuela says seeing something big is like seeing close-up, and seeing close-up is seeing things as they truly are. The butterflies in the photographs are every bit as monstrous as the large bug the woman with the silver hair was holding.

When you see butterflies fluttering around the garden, they look smooth like paper, but close-up, they are creatures of texture. Their torsos are covered in coarse black hair, with large goggle eyes and tendrils curling out from the center of their faces. Only their wings are beautiful, an impossible maze of color, not smooth but with layers of scale. Abuela would say that it doesn't matter how beautiful the wings are, they mean nothing without the more practical parts.

With each passing moment Mommy grows more tense, a flush has been slowly creeping into her ears, and now her entire face is red.

She keeps us moving with the line, but otherwise does not look up from her phone which chimes a new demand every few seconds. I think she is texting Daddy, and I want her to take a picture of us and send it to him, but I've learned not to ask about Daddy these days.

I saw Daddy last night. He explained why Abuela couldn't see the new Butterfly House with me. He told me she had to go back home to the rainforest where she used to live when she was a girl my age and that she is now a beautiful blue butterfly soaring free through the canopy of trees.

On our last visit to the Botanical Gardens, Abuela told me about her home, about how the rain rattled through leaves so thick it could take days to reach the ground, and about bright little snakes weaving their long bodies amongst the vines. Most of all she talked about butterflies as large as birds fluttering across the forest floor in swarms of blue. She called these the blue morphos, the most beautiful butterflies on Earth.

While I'm sad she never warned me she was leaving, I'm glad she's finally back where her heart was the happiest. I promised Daddy I'd look for one of those big blue butterflies and ask it to deliver a message to Abuela for us, telling her how much we love her and how badly she is missed. Abuela once told me butterflies can pass messages from one to the next all over the world, even if their wing colors don't quite match.

When it's finally our turn, we are told that we must wait for the door to close completely behind us before we can go all the way through. As the man with the shaggy beard explains, this is to prevent the butterflies from escaping and laying eggs that could damage our own local plants and animals. He says we must do the same thing when it is time to exit. I hope they are also trying to protect the butterflies. How sad it would be for one to escape and find herself out in a strange meadow with no others of her kind, but I'm also worried I will not be able to send a message to Abuela like I promised Daddy. Just as we are about to go through the first set of doors, I tell the man with the shaggy beard my problem, how I need a butterfly to deliver an important message to Costa Rica.

When he smiles, I check his eyes, which look small behind the thick lenses of his glasses and know he is safe and cheerful like Daddy. "That is no problem at all," he reassures me. "You need to find yourself a good old monarch butterfly in one of the gardens outside."

"Monarchs fly all the way down to Mexico," he explains, lecturing loud enough for the crowd around us to hear, "and will carry your message almost the entire way. Central America is filled with local butterflies who would be happy to relay your message from the monarchs to the morphos. So, don't worry, the butterflies have you covered." He laughs. He attaches a sticker of an orange and black butterfly to the lace of my dress so I will recognize them when I am exploring outside. Some people laugh at me, but I know they are not trying to be mean because their smiles shoot straight into their eyes.

"Harper, honey, you're holding up the line," Mommy scolds through clenched teeth. I'm about to get my second warning and so fall silent. Mommy peels the sticker from my dress with the tip of her fingernail. "Sorry." she says, "but this expensive little dress needs to make it through both a holiday and a wedding."

The greenhouse is like I imagined Costa Rica to be. Trees soar upwards, their wooden fingers threatening to break through the fragile glass ceiling and into the world beyond. Red flowers hang from vines draped just beyond reach. Birds the color of ice-cream swoop back and forth, screeching angrily at the people crowding their domain below. Even Mommy puts her phone away. Gazing upwards in wonder at water falling from someplace near the top of the greenhouse, her blue eyes seem to dance against the shimmering cascade. Smiling tightly at the other mothers as they set their children free to run, Mommy unstraps me from the stroller. Grabbing Teddy, I head down the wooden pathway into the wall of green. My shiny white shoes pinch my toes, but I enjoy the clunky sounds they make as I cross the footbridge.

At first, it takes a few seconds to notice the butterflies amongst these other worlds, but they are resting on every plant, brightly colored wings opening and closing in the hot sun. A flurry of butterflies with wings striped like tigers vie for nectar amongst a patch of crimson flowers, while a butterfly with wings as clear as windowpanes poses on a wooden post, collecting the admiration of passing visitors.

Sweat gathers under my arms and under the ribbon at my waist, and I'm drawn towards the coolness of the falling water. It's here that I find the blue ones, the morphos, fluttering heavily through the mist, each a piece of bright blue sky against a waterfall cloud. When one lands on a broad leaf, I'm surprised to discover that the underside of its wing is brown with red and yellow circles. The circles look like monster eyes, the sorts of eyes which peak out from the shadows under the bed, eyes meant to scare rather than to see. The contrast is so startling, I almost drop Teddy into the water, and it is only because a nice girl catches him that he is safe.

"Is this what Abuela looks like now?" I wonder.

I look down into the fountain to see where Teddy would have gone had he fallen. The current churns with wings of all colors mixing in the foam.

Suddenly, my entire body starts weeping for Abuela. Tears pour into my hair and down my back. Only my eyes are dry. "I cannot cry," I tell myself. "I cannot get my second warning."

The world spins as an oversized butterfly from one of photographs casts its shadow over me, its long tendril wheedling its way in through my ear and into my brain. My head fills with the fluttering of wings as my vision blurs and narrows. "I have a message," it whispers in a voice far too soft to be Abuela. "Your Abuela is now part of the great love that is eternity." I do not know what this means. All I know is that Abuela has gone beyond where even the butterflies can travel, and I will never see her again.

I hear a little girl screaming in the distance, and it is a moment before I realize that the screaming child is me. I am crying for Abuela, for Daddy, for my other Grandma, but it is Mommy who comes, her sharp heels echoing across the uneven path. "Look what you've done!" she scolds, her eyes filled with shards of ice.

I'm drenched clear through the special dress, the yellow fabric hangs stained and limp. Not only am I covered with sweat, but I've also wet myself, pee running down my stockings and into my shoes. "You ruin everything!" Mommy shouts, forgetting the people who are watching. "This is your second warning!"

She grabs me by the arm, pulling me painfully down the path. I've dropped Teddy, but she will not let me go back for him. Losing Teddy will be my punishment for getting my second warning. She shoves me into the stroller, crouching down to look me in the eye, close enough for me to smell the sweet stench of perfume intermingling with sweat. Her hair has gone limp in the humidity of the Butterfly House, and mascara trickles from her eyes in black rivulets. She no longer looks like one of the angels from the church, but like someone desperate, stranded in this place where she never wanted to be.

"I hate you," she hisses, hot breath burrowing into my ear. "I hate you."

The Magic of the Moonshinestill (Rocky Top Distilled Through the Mind of My Younger Self)

by Joshua Balog

Joshua Balog (they/them) is a Gen X neurodivergent genderqueer physical manifestation of whimsy. They currently reside in Washington, DC, and in a state of perpetual curiosity. Joshua spent 20 years in the US Army as a photographer/videographer and traveled extensively. They enjoy watching The Great British Baking Show *and professional wrestling.*

When I was a kid
Growing up in Tennessee
I heard the song "Rocky Top" a lot
It's one of the state songs of Tennessee
(by the way, did you know that Tennessee has ten state songs?
That's more than any other state)
(Also, if you don't know the song
The rest of this will make very little sense)
Great song, very catchy,
Traditionally sung at football games

Anyway

I had zero idea what the lyrics were about
The girl who was half bear/half cat sounded awesome
Being wild and sweet seemed like really excellent qualities
I had no clue what a mink was, but I loved soda pop
I was left with an image of this wildsweet dreamgirl monster
Like if Dolly Parton was a werewolf
But you know, bear and cat instead of wolf
So, a werebearcat, I guess?

Anyway

The part of "Rocky Top" that always got me
Was the part where I now know the song is actually talking about
Tax revenuers trying to find where people were making illegal alcohol
And getting killed by the folks who were making it
But I was just a little kid, I didn't know about any of that stuff
I mean, I didn't even understand the part about telephone bills
I thought it was "ain't no telephone bells"
Meaning that the phones on Rocky Top didn't ring
I thought that was kind of strange, but in my mind
Rocky Top was a very strange place

Anyway

In the song, two strangers climb Rocky Top
"Looking for a moonshine still"
I fixated on that phrase; it took hold of me
The only moonshine I knew was the literal light from the actual moon
Adding "still" to it somehow made it sound mystical and unreal
I imagined two wizards
Going to the top of this faerie mountain
With silent phones and bearcat girls
And at the peak of Rocky Top
There must have been a mirrorcalm pond
And when the moon shone on it
In just the right way
On just the right night
The light was so perfect and pure
And reflected from the pond to the moon
And back again
And just for an instant
There would be a magic silvergold stillness
An undiluted peace
Unlike anything else in the world
And maybe these two wizards
Wanted to capture that gleaming luminescence
To work some great and fearsome enchantment
But maybe the bearcat girl
Was a powerful fairy, or a witch, or both
Who protected the pond and the
Magic of the Moonshinestill
And maybe that is why
The wizards never came down

And we reckon they never will

Anyway

When I got older, and I learned what moonshine was
And how it was made in a still
The song lost a lot of its charm
Especially since I'm not really into football
But if I'm in the right mood
I can forget what I've learned
And let myself go back
To the brilliant magical land of
Rocky Top, Tennessee
And hear the story of the two wizards
Trying to capture moonlight

I Saw Faces in a Cornfield

by Jack Moran

Jack Moran is a graduate of Toledo School of the Arts, where he studied poetry and creative writing under Mark Allred and Justin Longacre for three years. He spends his free time fishing, golfing, caddying, playing guitar, and reading poetry about the outdoors. He was previously published by Of Rust and Glass in 2020 and finds inspiration from nature. He loves to write about his time in Boy Scouts, where he earned his Eagle Rank. He looks forward to studying Medicine at Ohio State in the fall and plans to continue writing wherever life takes him.

I saw faces in a corn field
Just off the highway
In Grand Rapids
Between the tall stalks
Of a midnight corn maze
Ears of every size
Are hidden by husks
Of golden hair and brown curls
Made up of the
People who plant the
Fields all around

I saw faces of
The people I know
People who muddy their
Ford floor mats with
Boots caked in sand dunes
Just for a chance to see
The dancing lights of Alaska
From the great 48
The people who learned
To listen for wind in pine needles
And keep a picnic
Blanket in their trunk

I saw the face of a bassist
Made famous from gravel pit parties
And basement noise shows

At a college in Ohio
A bassist whose prayer is nights spent
Bent over a Kroger bag
Shucking corn
At a homeless shelter in Cleveland
The same shelter fishing philanthropists
Leave a legal limit of walleye
On the doorstep
Every Monday

I saw the faces of
The American lifeblood
The faces who cry and bleed
The blood sweat and tears
Intertwined with the roots
Of the apple trees and grape vines
Of a west coast Michigan
Winery
But also every wire
In a supermarket parking lot
Light pole in Illinois
The same Walmart where
The wrangler shopping scooter first debuted

I saw the faces of every person
I'll never meet
Who live around me in
The waterways and wrecked
Farmhouses
Found between the open plains
Of Oklahoma and the right side of the rustbelt
I saw faces in a cornfield once
But I just threw my empty apple core
Out the sunroof and kept driving

Message in a Bottle

by Mitch James

Mitch James is a Professor of Composition and Literature at Lakeland Community College in Kirtland, OH and the Managing Editor at Great Lakes Review. *His first novel* Seldom Seen *is forthcoming with Sunbury Press in the fall of 2022. You can find his latest short fiction in* Made of Rust and Glass: Midwest Literary Fiction Vol. 2, Red Branch Review, *and* Bull, *poetry at* Watershed Journal, I Thought I Heard a Cardinal Sing: Ohio's Appalachian Voices, *and* Southern Florida Poetry Journal, *and scholarship at* Journal of Creative Writing Studies. *Find more of his work at mitchjamesauthor.com and follow him on Twitter @mrjames5527.*

Donovan's the one that found the bottle, stepped on it, nearly busted his ass. We were on our way home from school. It was half sunk in the ground. We were going to leave it, but he said, "Eh, there's somethin' in there." It was a folded piece of paper, brown and creased all over like an old map. We tried to shake it free, then dig it out with a stick, then decided we'd get tweezers from the trailer. I put the bottle in my bag, and we went to my place. Outside, I set the bottle below my bedroom window, then we went in.

Laura was up and around. You never could be sure. I said, "Hi, mom," and she rubbed my head and said hi to Donovan and asked what we were about to get into as she lit a Pall Mall. I said, "We're gonna go study for a science test," and she said, "Like hell." She asked if we were going to do drugs. I said, "You ask us every week," and she said, "Just waitin' for the right answer." She cackled and rubbed my head again. "Let me see your bags," and she helped them off our shoulders. She propped them on the recliner and went through them. "I smoked weed at twelve," she stated. She always seemed disappointed she didn't find anything. "You tell momma if you're about to get into somethin'. I've done it all and'll steer ya right." "I won't, mom," I said, not about telling but about not doing the drugs. She said, "Oh, you're gonna. Might as well be straight with me."

I wouldn't and there were reasons, John being one. He'd be gone for months, then come home long enough to tell Laura he was sorry and smack her around and help himself to her pills. The other was because I'd seen Laura pass out with a cigarette in broad day and set her clothes on fire, and I hear her moving about the house at all hours, never knowing when she'll sleep or wake. Sometimes I come home from school and she's in her chair the same way she was when I left, and I think she's dead, and If I'm being honest, I never know what to do. Whether or not to try and wake her. And this is why I'll never do drugs, not weed or meth or even those fucking pills. Especially not the pills.

Back in my room, I pulled the bottle through the window and faked going to the bathroom so I could get tweezers. It was tough to get the paper out without tearing it, but I managed. Donovan and I looked at each other like we knew we were about to embark on something big, like maybe we were both asking the other not to open it, and I said, "You ready?" and he said, "Go for it."

It read: "It'll all be okay. Just wait. I'll come for you."

"That's it?" asked Donovan. "Yeah," I said. Donovan said, "Ain't that some bullshit?" "Y'all watch yer fuckin' mouths," Laura ordered from the hall. The bathroom door shut and toilet seat slapped. "No name. No map to a million dollars," Donovan started again in a whisper. "Map to a million dollars? You're an idiot." "Man, we hauled that bottle all the way here for that." I said, "It ain't no thang. Just put it in my bag." "Shoulda been a not-thang we left in the woods." He stared at it like he might take it or break it or throw it, and I don't know why, but I felt I shouldn't let him. "Yeah, kinda a waste of time, but not a big deal," and I took the bottle and note and pitched them in the wastebasket.

Donovan stayed until we didn't hear Laura moving around, then we went to the kitchen, and I gave him a pack of ramen and a coffee filter of Captain Crunch with a rubber band around it, and I made him a peanut butter sandwich and put it all in a plastic grocery bag. By spreading it out like that, Laura wouldn't know I gave Donovan food. He left by the light of a cataract moon, and I went back to my room, where I cleaned the old brown bottle and read the note again and again.

***

I woke with the note in my hand and hid it and the bottle in my closet. That week I looked everywhere for whoever wrote the note. I felt foolish, even then, but I felt something else too. Maybe hope? When I saw feet in the stalls of the boys' bathroom, I'd wait for whoever was there to call my name or say something to me in code, like maybe recite part of the note and see if I could finish it. I took as many bathroom breaks as I could so I could walk the halls and check around corners. I got sent back to homeroom with the threat of detention for snooping in a maintenance closet. I even looked in the sink drain. I just felt there was an answer to the note, even though I didn't know what the answer was, human or spirit or just a feeling of something that would make me feel different in a good way.

At first, I only thought about the bottle, thought about going home to see if it was still there, see if Laura had found it or the note. After school, Donovan and I would play. We'd hit the skate park when there was no snow in winter and in the spring would take the bikes to Bedford Reservation. If he was having a bad day, which usually meant Liam, his stepdad, had whipped him across the back of his thighs with an extension cord, we'd go to A&M or Giant Eagle, and I'd play blind shopper and harass others, pull items from shelves and ask if they were things they weren't. I'd knock things on the floor. Once people got agitated enough, employees would come to throw me out while not paying attention to Donovan, who'd be in some other part of the store stealing stuff. We'd meet outside and ride to City View Center, to the abandoned Walmart. There was a storage closet in the back of the building, and he'd put what he stole in a paper towel box we called the treasure chest.

When Liam started getting drunk early, Donovan knew it would get bad if he didn't pass out before dinner. On one such night, Donavan slipped out to my house with blankets and a bag of clothes and said he was running away and wanted to know if he could stay with me. Laura would've never known, but John was home then, so I said no but snuck out with my own gear, and we rode to City View Center. Ever since, that closet had become our home away from home. We put shit on the shelves, and the faucet still worked, which we couldn't believe, somebody payin' water to the whole place. We'd stay over a couple of nights a month and read comics by the light of candles Donovan stole from the Dollar Tree while I made a mess out of an aisle on the other side of the store.

After a while, the pull of the bottle became too much. I started thinking of it being alone, like maybe whoever was supposed to come make things alright might show up and I not be there. I thought a couple of times that maybe whoever it was would kill my family, that that's the way they intended to help. I didn't feel too guilty about the thought at first. I even thought hard about what Laura would look like dead. I pictured her looking like she did when I found her mid-day and wasn't sure if she was alive or sleeping. It was easy to visualize what she'd look like dead, seeing it so often. But after a while, I did start to feel guilty, thinking of seeing her dead. I felt like a better person for feeling guilty. But I also knew that if whoever came for the bottle said killing Laura was the way to save me, I'd probably let them. I'd ask to leave the house, or at least the room, but I wouldn't try and stop them.

I started leaving Donovan at school, making excuses why I couldn't hang out. He tried to come with, but I told him he couldn't. At first, I lied and said John was back home and lit up and slapping Laura around again. But when it appeared John had stayed longer than usual, Donovan came by the house unannounced, asked Laura if John was around, said he had some questions about some spinnerbait he was thinking about picking up, and Laura told him he hadn't seen that prick in nine months. Donovan came back to my room long enough to call me a fucking liar. And a twat. I hit his mouth, and we tumbled through the lauan bedroom door, and Laura hit us with the handle of the broom. Donovan was on top of me. He could've caused damage. My throat was in his hand, and his fist was cocked back, and Laura was cracking him across the shoulders with the broom handle, and he said, "Where's yer friend now, huh? Yer fucking friend from the bottle gonna save ya now?" But he never hit me. He just snatched the broom from Laura mid-swing, tossed it on the couch, and left. Laura asked if all that was over a woman. I said, "Yeah." There was a proud nod. Then she asked what was the deal with the friend from the bottle? She wanted to know if it was code for drugs and, if so, to let her know because she'd done them all and could steer me right. I ignored her and went to my room.

I started taking the bottle to school with me. I couldn't stomach the thought of leaving it. Then I stopped going to school altogether. I stayed home with the bottle, waiting for whoever wrote the message. Donavan came over two more times. On the second, he asked if I wanted to ride bikes, see if I wanted to go to City View Center, said I could even bring the stupid fucking bottle, but I said no, and when he asked why, I didn't even have an answer. I gave him one, a lie. I don't even remember what it was. I just wanted to be there, alone with the bottle and whatever it might summon to save me.

Donavan never returned. Laura could be found dotting different parts of the house, half-conscious most times. Other times, she'd come to check on me, see what I was up to. When checking my book bag for the third time in four days, I told her I hadn't left, that there was nothing new in the bag, and that if I were going to hide something, it wouldn't be there. She threw the bag and started tearing clothes from my drawers, stripping piles of stuff from the closet. "Where is it!" she belted. "Where is it!" When I asked her what, she said the drugs. She said cops came by to report my absences from school. She said she'd stuck up for me, made it so I could have a few more days at home. "It didn't matter if it was the law! I stood for you, my son! And this is how you repay me. Where's it at! I know a drug user when I see one." And I thought, *I bet you do, you dumb bitch. I bet you do.* But I didn't say it. Then, she pulled at my foot. "Get out of that bed. I'm flipping the mattress." When I shook my foot free, she started yanking at blankets. There was a rattle as the bottle bounced through the bars of the headboard. "What's that!" We grabbed the bottle at the same time. She tugged. "Stop it," I ordered. "Don't you fucking tell me to stop it, boy!" She slapped me across the face. Pulled the bottle. When I didn't let go, she slapped me again. "I carried your rotten ass around for nine months." She worked her palm across my face a third time. "Brought you into this world." And a fourth.

"Let go," I warned. When she pulled again, I stood and shoved her to the ground. I had never seen her so afraid. I'd seen her smile at men who brought ham fists to her mouth. She looked up at me, from me to the bottle and back. "No. No! Just like your father! Just like your grandpa, oh Christ!" She could hardly crawl over herself fast enough. I heard her scuttle across the linoleum in the hall, rolling herself up in her muted fragments and sheer cries shrill as razor wire. I found great strength in the bottle. I thought maybe I was finding answers too, though I wasn't certain to what.

Though I had lied about John, he did return, not even a week after I pushed Laura. They argued his first day back, as always, and screwed all night. In the morning he gave me a talk about pushing on Laura, but he knew he had no right. Plus, he knew when I got older, I'd whip his ass, and so he was starting to grease the wheels even then. Treating me a little more like an equal. Hell, it almost seemed there was pride in his eyes, like he was seeing something in me he was worried he'd never see but was glad he did.

A few nights after he came home, John was drinking and crossing pills and started hitting on Laura. He wasn't trying to end her. We all knew the difference. It was more like when a cat plays with its prey. He'd slap her. Push her. Let her wrestle back. Eventually, I knew it'd overflow, and he'd almost kill her and then leave again. Some nights, while listening, I'd think, just get to it already. Get it over with and get the hell out of here. Other times, I'd whisper to the bottle, "Now's the time. Time to come help me. What can I do? Have I done somethin' wrong?" I'd read the paper over and over again. I stopped whispering and would just hold the bottle to my chest and think, *please. I'm ready. How much longer do I have to wait?*

Then came the fight that'd been building for two weeks. John cracked his first beer while scooping coffee into the hopper. They picked at each other all day. You could feel the swell of tension between the two of them. It filled the whole trailer. Before sunset, words turned to wounds. Flesh on flesh. Broken glass. Holes in walls. I was in bed clutching the bottle. Thinking it was time. Thinking, *if not now, when? What's it gonna take?* There was yelling and then a loud thump. I felt the vibration of it through the bed frame. It was a body hitting the floor, and so I listened. As long as they were fighting, Laura was okay. But it was quiet. No yelling. Nothing breaking. Then I heard it, the smallest choke, a release of air through a pinched throat. He usually let her breathe every few seconds when he choked her, so I started counting to myself, to the bottle. 1...2...3...When I didn't hear anything at five, I walked through the hall, to the living room. He was over Laura, both hands around her throat. His back was wide like wings and flexed with effort. He did not hear me walk up. I brought the bottom of the bottle down where his head sat on his neck. He grunted and turned to look, and I brought the bottle against his ear. When he leaned away, I brought it into his nose, across his lip, where a tooth chipped and split through. From his back, he kicked me in the gut, and I flew like a toy into the wall. My stomach was a deflated balloon of dense pain that could not take air. My mouth moved like a fish out of water. It made no sound. He threw the bottle at me but missed. It shattered against a door frame. I thought I might suffocate. Laura did not move. I could not tell if she was alive or dead.

Suddenly, I began inhaling small envelopes of air as John rose. He grinned. Pulling his lip back over his tooth, he said, "There he is. I've been waitin' for you, boy. Been watin' and hopin'. Wonderin' what it was gonna take." Looking at the folded paper amongst the glass, he asked, "Now, what's this?" I stretched my arm toward it, but he stepped on my hand and took the paper from the floor. He unfolded it and chuckled. "Well, ain't that somethin'. Boy, whatever you think is comin' is already here. This," he said, turning to the trailer in disarray, turning to look at Laura on the floor, "this is all the help you'll ever need. This'll make ya ready for anything." He let my hand free and turned and said, "It's the only kinda help people like us get." Laura shifted her legs and groaned. "You're welcome," he said, wadding the paper in his fist and pinning it to his bleeding ear.

Whatnot

by Rikki Santer

Rikki Santer's poetry has received many honors including six Pushcart and three Ohioana and Ohio Poet book award nominations as well as a fellowship from the National Endowment for the Humanities. Her eleventh poetry collection, Stopover, which is in conversation with the original Twilight Zone series, was recently published by Luchador Press. She is also a member of the teaching artist roster of the Ohio Arts Council, a vice president of the Ohio Poetry Association, and a member of the poetry troupe Concrete Wink. Please contact her through her website: rikkisanter.com

When leatherback sea turtles
   surrender and
tactical diagrams regret,

bear head sketches snatch
   8 million dollars and
homeless can't imagine any more.

Anne Frank memes
   turn turgid, plastic
Buddhas bob in sewage drains.

Poems testify for defense
   in murder trials and
hurricanes revolt against their nicknames.

Raw data overcooked to serve
   assumptions, lamppost
moons refuse to temper their tongues.

Before technology goes any further.
   before time gets out of joint.
Knock knock Who's there?

Push back your slack jaw and
   jury-rig your saffron heart
for not this, not that in minor key.

The Girl with the Red Umbrella

by Steve Cain

Steve Cain is a native of Augusta, Georgia and has lived in the Cincinnati area since 2015. A safety and environmental manager by day, Steve has published twelve books and poetry and short stories and one horror novel, Thorn. *His story, "'Til the Well Runs Dry," was featured in Of Rust and Glass' Fall 2021 edition, and another story, "The Girl with the Red Umbrella," was included in the Spring 2022 issue. A singer/songwriter, as well, Steve's vocals can be found on the 2021 CD by Rising Within. He is married with two kids, a cat, and two dogs.*

Lorelei awoke to another dreary, rainy day. Every day was like that. Every day. It had been six months since her mother passed away. Her best friend and confidant. The person she admired most, who brought sunshine to the world. Now, there was only rain.

She got out of her black bed, went to her black bathroom, and sat on her black toilet. When she was finished, she dropped her black nightgown to the floor, got into her black shower, and turned on the cold, black water. She scrubbed herself from head to toe with black soap, rinsed off with the black water, and dried off with a black towel.

Lorelei slipped into a black dress and made herself a black coffee in a black mug. The coffee was hot, and as it went down her throat into her stomach, it felt like love. She wrinkled her nose and emptied the mug into the black sink.

Disgusted with herself, and with life itself, Lorelei put on her black shoes, picked up her black umbrella from the black stand in the corner, removed her black keys from the black hook on the black wall, and opened her black door, flipping the black lock as she left. She didn't know why she had bothered to lock the door; she had no plans to come back to her black home. She was going out to say goodbye.

Outside, the sky was gray. Gray rain fell from gray clouds. As she walked, her shoes *squeak-squeaked* on the gray sidewalk. Gray cars passed her on the gray street. One car beeped its horn, and even that sounded gray. A gray cat crossed in front of her into a gray yard. It didn't bother to look her way.

At an intersection, Lorelei stopped at a gray stop sign and crossed the road to the left when it was safe. That was ironic, considering, but that's not how she wanted it done. She stepped onto the gray bridge and made her way to the top of its gray arc. There, she peered down into the gray, flowing river, watching as the gray raindrops pitter-pattered the surface and were swept downstream. Yes, this was right. This was the way, but not yet. She still had to say goodbye.

Lorelei continued across the bridge, and the other side was less populated as she had expected. There were no gray cars, no gray cats, just gray trees and gray grass. She made another left down a gray dirt road and passed between gray iron gates. She stepped around gray puddles, which also seemed ironic. *Afraid to get wet?* she asked herself, shaking her head. At the next gray puddle, Lorelei stomped, splashing gray water and gray mud onto her white gray skin. She stomped at the next puddle, too. And the next. Further down the road, at another puddle, she jumped with both feet, making a large *sploosh*, sending mud and water onto her dress, face, and hair. She almost smiled, then marched on, stoically. There were no more smiles, no more fun, no more happiness.

Here and there, off the gray dirt road, in the gray grass, beneath the gray trees, under the gray sky, were gray marbled headstones: *Fullington, Monroe, Isley, Barlow.* Lorelei passed them all. She didn't know them. She stopped at the base of a short, gray hill and stepped into the wet, gray grass. She climbed slowly. There was no need to hurry.

At the top of the hill, beneath a gray oak tree stood two gray stones: *Beloved Father, Beloved Mother.* She had made peace with her father's passing. It had been so long ago, and she hardly remembered his face. Gray moss grew on the front of his gray tombstone. She reached out but did not touch his stone.

Lorelei looked instead to her mother's grave. The gray dirt still formed a slight gray mound, as it had not fully settled. The headstone was new and smooth. She ran a white hand across the top of the gray stone, across *Beloved Mother,* across her mother's name: *Julia.*

The gray rain continued, but she the gray oak leaves kept her dry. Lorelei closed her black umbrella and set it against the trunk of the gray tree. She had thought about this moment, thought of what she wanted to say, had practiced her speech into her black mirror. Now, the words wouldn't come. Black tears filled her black eyes, and she cleared her throat. "Mother…"

It didn't matter, anyway. If her mother was in Heaven, she knew what Lorelei meant to say. She knew it was goodbye, at least for her here. Lorelei hoped God would grant her mercy and let her be with her mother soon. Her father, too.

Lorelei turned and took two steps away from the grave, two steps that left her unprotected by the gray leaves. Gray rain pelted her, and she turned back to retrieve her black umbrella. To her surprise, it was no longer standing at the base of the tree where she had placed it. She walked around the tree, but it wasn't there. She looked down both sides of the gray hill, thinking perhaps it had fallen over and rolled down the hill. Nothing.

It doesn't matter, Lorelei thought. *I'm going to be very wet soon, anyway.* With a sigh, she trudged down the hill without looking back at the graves. At the bottom, she turned and started back down the gray dirt road. She passed through the gray iron gates, towards the gray bridge. As she reached the bridge and ascended the arc, the place where she would say goodbye for the last time, the gray clouds separated, and a yellow sun peeked through. The rain slowed and stopped. There, against the gray railing, at the very spot where she intended to jump, Lorelei found an umbrella leaning against the gray steel. It was not her black umbrella. This one was red, her mother's favorite color. Julia's favorite color.

Lorelei lifted the umbrella, and it felt warm in her hands. That warmth spread up her arm, across her face, and down into her chest. It was like the coffee in her stomach, but it wasn't black.

The rain had stopped, but Lorelei opened the umbrella anyway. The sun broke through the clouds then, the yellow orb filling the now blue skies. Lorelei looked down at her dress, watching as the black melted away, replaced by white, with yellow and brown sunflowers printed on the fabric. The black on her shoes faded to reveal mud-soaked, but otherwise white high-tops. She saw the bridge's purple splendor, and the azure water in the river below rushed past as she watched, astounded. A trio of brown otters swam by, playing what looked to be a game of tag. A magnificent white duck with her orange bill and orange webbed feet waddled down the down the bank in the green grass, yellow ducklings following behind her, single file. Somewhere nearby, a baby laughed, and it was the sound of pure happiness, perhaps the greatest sound she had ever heard. The world had color again, and Lorelei was warm for the first time in six months. She allowed herself to smile, and her face regained its rosy-beige complexion.

Lorelei reached into her pocket to find a tissue. Her hand rested on her keys, which she realized she would need after all. With the umbrella open above her head, red and vibrant in the midday sun, Lorelei took her first steps out of her gray and black world into a world of color and hope. She could smile again. She could be happy again, and not feel ashamed. She wouldn't look at her mother's face today, but she knew her mother was looking down upon her. There would be many more rainy days, but Lorelei, the girl with the red umbrella, knew there would be more sunny days too.

Two Poems
by Jessica Weyer Bentley

Jessica Weyer Bentley's first collection of poetry, Crimson Sunshine, *was published in May 2020 by AlyBlue Media. She has contributed work to several publications for the Award-Winning Book Series,* Grief Diaries, *including* Poetry and Prose *and* Hit by a Drunk Driver. *Jessica's work has been anthologized in* Women Speak Vol. 6 *(Sheila-Na-Gig Editions),* Summer Gallery of Shoes *(Highland Park Poetry),* Common Threads 2020 Edition *(Ohio Poetry Association),* Appalachian Witness Volume 24 *(Pine Mountain Sand and Gravel),* Made and Dream *(Of Rust and Glass), and* Psalms of the Alien Buddha Part 2. *Her work has also appeared in online blogs including* Global Poemic *and* Fevers of the Mind Poetry Showcase 2022. *She is a 2022* Fevers of the Mind Wolfpack Poet Contributor.*

Janie

What have we grown,
as we have grown old,
our promise in this sun-kissed frame,
never afraid,
pushing hard against this world of asphalt.
She softens it somehow,
revealing a hue of integrity,
of humanity,
in a world angry,
agitated,
brazen in black.
Her aura of seafoam and blue,
breaking through leaving a crack for change.
A mermaid breaking the wake,
revealing herself to the crew.
She rearranges our upbringing,
turning it on its head,
marrying the old and new.
The perfect storm.
Rise up sweet girl.
Take the helm.

Paramour

I struggle to linger.
My mind softens-
a wood chip in winter.
The center oozes-
a half-baked cake.
I cannot heed to your indifference.
The fabric sings,
a desperate force.
This faded glass of champagne-
stale.
I lie inebriated,
saturating this white gown-
stained gold.
This veil has aged.
The lines deepen beneath my mascara.
I pleaded you in a whisper-
stay.
To give a glance,
a nod-
one word.
Peer at me with your cobalt gaze.
Let me live again.
Allow me to be born.

The Humbling River
by William Thatch

William Thatch is a 12-time published author of short stories in anthologies from Scout Media and Pixie Forest Publishing, and a novella published by Zombie Pirate Publishing. William attributes much of his ability to develop well-crafted, realistic characters to his lived experience facing seemingly insurmountable struggle, and his affinity for professional wrestling, which has afforded him employment as a transcriptionist. William is currently working on his first novel, tentatively titled The Wayward Son. *To find out more about William visit WilliamThatch.com or follow him on Twitter @IAmThatch.*

A thin layer of sweat on Maggie's forehead glistened in the moonlight as she lay on the couch. She had returned home from the hospital only a week after the accident. Her recovery had taken months, and it would take many more months to heal to the fullest extent that her body ever would. Between the inability to climb stairs by herself and no one considering how she would get up to her bedroom before she returned home, Maggie spent her nights in the living room.

As with most people, Maggie dreamed every night, and the majority of her dreams would go unnoticed. The ones that she noticed were unremarkable to the point she'd forget them that day— short films from which she was disconnected. Tonight, however, the dream replayed one of her favorite memories and one of the proudest moments of her life.

She had stopped in the local music store in search of a new release of Huey Lewis and the News when she noticed a fellow student, and her tutee, Chelsea, also looking at the rows of cassette tapes. Chelsea had endured a rough home life, and while Maggie had the decency not to ask for details, she could see the will to try for better had been figuratively beaten out of her. Maggie had been tutoring a few students who had trouble with various subjects. The high school's math teacher had pulled her aside one day to introduce her and Chelsea. It took a while to get Chelsea on the right track. She still wasn't an A-student, but Maggie had seen the young girl's pride when she began to understand the material and her grades improved.

By the time she'd found Chelsea at the music store, however, the material had grown too hard again and Maggie suspected Chelsea's home life had overwhelmed her self-confidence, leading to her quitting the lessons.

Maggie watched from between the aisles as Chelsea took covert glances up and down her aisle before slipping a cassette tape into her pocket and continued browsing as if nothing had happened. Maggie's heart sank as she watched her student fall back into her old habits. She had hope for Chelsea. She may not ever be the best student, but she was worth more as a person.

Light on her feet, Maggie moved around the end of the shelves and into the aisle with Chelsea, noting her younger brother Brandon standing by the glass windows.

Strange, Maggie noted. *He wasn't there that day.*

Maggie had neither the understanding nor the intention of stealth in her plan. She stepped right up in front of Chelsea, snatched a cassette off the rack and shoved it into her own pocket.

"What are you doing?" Chelsea asked in a hushed tone.

"Well, you gave up," Maggie replied. "Why shouldn't I?"

From there the dream did as dreams do and operated in a less than real manner. Though the two girls continued speaking, Maggie couldn't make out what they said. The feeling of the conversation remained—Maggie's insistence that if Chelsea was going to steal, then so was she; the feeling of terror if the shop owner caught them; Chelsea's gloomy outlook trying to insist it was all she would ever amount to and that Maggie had more to look forward to and, eventually, Chelsea agreeing to put the cassette back. As much as Chelsea had a reputation and did not care about hers anymore, she wasn't going to let Maggie damage her own.

That was the moment Maggie was proudest of, the moment she had gotten Chelsea back on the right path. It was also the point in which Chelsea, having always kept Maggie at arm's length emotionally, was forced to acknowledge they were friends. Maggie's dream had edited out the hug at the end, much to her disappointment.

Maggie slipped the cassette out of her pocket and glanced to see what she had bluffed Chelsea with. The moment her eyes left Chelsea, however, the mood inside the store changed. Chelsea had disappeared along with everyone else. Although the store's lights remained on, Maggie got the distinct impression it was dark, and a sense of dread carried on the night winds which passed by her. Her mind had shifted to a different memory; a different night. A night she was less inclined to reminisce about.

Instinctively, Maggie turned towards her brother. Tires squealed nearby and her breath caught in her lungs. A truck appeared behind Brandon, the headlights blinding her, reducing Brandon to a silhouette.

"Brandon!" she screamed, praying it would be enough to avert the dream ending as the night actually had.

Instead, the dream came to its end as Maggie sat upright on the living room couch. A thin layer of sweat covered her as her scream transferred into the real world. The change of scenery caught her off guard for a moment before her emotions caught up to her. A few short gasps preceded the only expression she could muster; a long, loud wail of grief as warm tears journeyed down her face.

Her cries stuttered and she sucked in more air for the next wail, drowning out the footsteps in the house closing in on her. Her mother, Margaret, had appeared from the lit-up kitchen, speckled with flour and smelling of vanilla extract while her father, Brian, came charging down the stairs as he pulled his arm through the sleeve of his robe. Maggie broke down into a series of smaller wails as she gasped for enough air when her parents reached her and pulled the entire family—what was left of it—into an embrace.

Not one of the Morris family needed an explanation as to why. Her parents had managed their grief in a reserved manner, losing themselves in baking or the congregation. Maggie shook uncontrollably as she spotted the metallic bits of her wheelchair in the glint of the moonlight—a solemn reminder of the toll the wreck had taken on her and that neither of the Morris children had walked away from the crash.

For as long as Maggie could remember, the Morris family had been a pillar of the community. She recognized it from an early age, watching as the citizens of Riverton, Wyoming flocked to the Crossroads Inspirational Fellowship church every Sunday, congregating in the nave attached to the house. People would go so far as to call on Brian Morris, the town's pastor, midweek if their problems became too much for them. She understood her family's importance to the community, being the conduit to God, responsible for teaching the word of the Bible to the masses.

Her mother Margaret stayed at home to raise Maggie and Brandon and had unofficially served as a marriage counselor and babysitter for those who needed it. It was through helping her mother watch the children in her teenage years that Maggie had transitioned into watching the young children during church hours. She had taken great pride when the parents had thanked her and recognized her not simply as the daughter of Brian and Margaret, the patriarch and matriarch of the community, but as her own person within the church, separate from her parents. Through her acknowledgement within the church, she had the school administration's confidence and trust to recommend her for tutoring students like Chelsea.

For all the good the church had reciprocated for her doing good, ever since Maggie had gotten out of the hospital, something had been missing on Sunday mornings. Although the doctors had given the go ahead to go home, she did not feel strong. Physically, she had always been on the dainty side. Brandon had relished the ability to lift things his sister couldn't as he got older. She never felt weak, even while acknowledging she needed a hand with heavier objects. But since the crash, there was not a day that she *did not* feel weak.

With few exceptions, Maggie had never missed church, and the fact that the church was not wheelchair-accessible had not deterred her. Every morning, her father would ease her down the steps of the stage, and after every congregation, he would bring her back up. Maggie could do little more than hold on and pray that he did not drop her. Every day, she would wheel herself off to the side, a little out of the way but without anyone accusing her of hiding.

None of it felt right anymore. At the end of service, her father would meet with the people who lingered, shaking hands, and catching up.

"How are you holding up, Brian?" they would ask.

Maggie knew her father. She could see in the way his chest rose that he had a lot to get off his chest about how his children's condition weighed on him. But he would never unload any of that weight on the people that relied on *him* to carry the weight of *their* burdens. So as always, her father would smile and nod.

"We're surviving," he would say.

Maggie assumed, as parents crossed through the hallway into the Morris' home, that they would have similar conversations with her mother, and that her mother would deftly change the topic from her own children to the kids in her care.

Rarely did anyone come to Maggie and inquire. When they did, it was awkward. Asking how she was with a pity smile. At best no one knew what to say, and at worst someone would try making conversation that Maggie had no interest in. Ordinarily, she loved the meet and greet, the catch up, bragging about how the little ones were coming along. Now she had nothing to say.

She felt nothing as she sat in the church today. As her eyes panned the familiar faces and felt nothing, she made sure to avoid the effigies of Christ around the nave. Maggie remained like this until the congregation had finally reached its conclusion, at which point her father helped her back up the stairs and into the house.

When she wasn't babysitting, Maggie's days had consisted of reading fiction or being a social butterfly around town, visiting with and talking to anyone she would pass. She knew some people spent the day sat in front of the television, and she could never understand those who shut out their community for hours at a time like that. Sure, like most people, Maggie would enjoy some of the primetime sitcoms—the dramas were a bit too heavy-handed for her tastes—but the daytime television felt a lot like people who found themselves swimming in alcohol to cope and hide.

Yet, these days, Maggie found herself sat with the living room curtains drawn and staring absently into the television set, her eyes glazed over in disinterest. Some days a couple of hours would go by and, when her mother would ask her what she was watching, Maggie genuinely couldn't say. It had so little entertainment or informational value it went in one ear and out the other. But there she sat in the warm, distracting glow, having just finished back-to-back episodes of the Madam Tatum show, a psychic guessing at details of call-in's lives.

"Maggie!" her mother called from the kitchen, "There's a call for you."

"Thank you," Maggie replied, her voice dulled and apathetic.

There had been a couple of calls here or there for her, but the thought of talking to someone was nauseating. She didn't want to hear the pity in people's voices, nor people who would try to act as if everything was normal. With practiced movement and never taking her eyes off the latest block of episodes of the Judge Eustace courtroom show, Maggie lifted the receiver and set it back down.

Maggie startled in her chair a few minutes later when her mother appeared beside her, smiling with her hands on her hips.

"I was thinking it's too beautiful of a day to spend cooped up inside," her mother said. "I was thinking about going down to the park. Would you like to come?"

It took Maggie a few seconds to reply. Not that she was thinking about how to respond or whether she wanted to. She didn't. But it was as if it took her brain some time to start up and register that she had been asked a question and needed to reply.

"Nah," Maggie said.

"Oh, come on. You don't want to be stuck inside all day," Margaret said, running her fingers through her daughter's shoulder-length dark brown hair. "I'll get your jacket and then we'll—"

Maggie grunted as her mother's slender fingers caught on, and ripped through, a few knots.

"We'll put your hair in a ponytail first and make a note to wash your hair later."

But how will I find out if this Elvis impersonator acted in self-defense or not? Maggie thought to herself, not convincing herself of the importance of this episode.

Margaret returned with a hair tie and wrangled the unwashed mop on Maggie's head into a ponytail, taking time to unknot more of her hair in the process.

When Margaret and Maggie arrived at the park, they chose a bench to sit and watch the children run and jump and play on the park's facilities.

"See, now isn't this better?" Margaret asked, scanning the children.

Maggie caught the subtle muscle twitch as her mother sucked in her inner cheek and lightly bit it. There was no doubt it all weighed on her parents as well. Brandon was twelve when he died in the wreck, far too old for the swing sets and slides, but still a child all the same.

"Margaret!" an elderly resident cried as she waved, her dachshund, Cinnamon, on a leash beside her.

"Oh, Gertrude!" Margaret said, patting the bench beside her, "Brian mentioned you weren't at church on Sunday."

"No, the little girl here—" Gertrude gestured to her dog as she sat down, "—got into the grand kid's toys at night and I took her to the vet. They said the marbles will pass eventually."

"Oh, dear."

Like that, the two women started catching up on what the other had been doing as of late and Maggie, once more, was left on the sidelines.

Maggie spent the time watching the children play, admiring the ones with the strength to handle the monkey bars and sympathizing with the ones who gave up a couple of rungs in. Maggie had almost made it across once when she was a kid, but she never managed all the way. At one point or another, Maggie had looked after all of these kids either in church or for general babysitting.

One of the children, Caleb, spent his time trying to walk up and then back down the slide, then he tried walking up one side of the seesaw and back down the other.

That child is going to hurt himself one of these days, Maggie thought to herself.

"Maggie!" cried out a shrill, tiny voice.

Turning her head, Maggie watched as a small blonde-haired child came running up to her and, without requesting, climbed into Maggie's lap to hug her. Out of the corner of her eye, Maggie watched as Mrs. Thompson was walking towards them, shaking her head at her daughter's running off.

"Hi, Laura!" Maggie said, smiling for the first time in months as she wrapped her arms around the child.

"Where were you, missy?" Laura asked, pulling away to put her balled up fists on her hips.

"I wasn't feeling well."

"Were you sick?"

"Kind of."

"Oh."

Laura gave Maggie another hug.

"What is new with you, little lady?" Maggie asked.

"I'm four now!" Laura exclaimed, showing five fingers.

Maggie politely folded in Laura's thumb so that she was only showing four fingers. Laura frowned at her hand as if it had betrayed her.

"Laura!" Mrs. Thompson said as she arrived, balling up her fists and placing them on her hips.

"What?" Laura asked, confused by the tone in her mother's voice.

"Come along, we're going to be late."

"Wait!" the child said, turning to Maggie. "Can I have a piggyback ride first?"

Maggie frowned as her heart sank. Laura always loved her piggyback rides. There hadn't been a single time—in church, during babysitting, or just general crossing paths—where the child had not asked for and received a piggyback ride.

"I'm sorry, Laura," Maggie said. "I can't anymore."

"Oh."

Laura's face fell. The child had no concept of the wheelchair, and most likely had not even noticed it. Mrs. Thompson said it was nice seeing Maggie again and scooped up Laura before continuing on her way.

Maggie's face turned towards her lap, the tears welling up in her eyes. With great restraint, she fought the tears off. Holding her breath in, she waited for the moment of emotions to pass before lifting her head back up and facing forward as her eyes glazed over once more.

Day after day and night after night played on repeat—time lost to the banality of daytime television, the evenings lost to sitcoms she no longer laughed at. Sundays were spent at service, stewing in the guilt of not wanting to be there. Everything she could do to avoid thinking about the crash, or Brandon, or her own situation.

The one day she felt up to doing something, she elected to go to the library on her own. After the terrifying drop off the front step at home, and the struggle to wheel herself to the library, she realized she had made a critical mistake—the library had a set of stairs leading up to it. An insurmountable challenge on wheels. Maggie had turned back home wondering how she was going to get up the front step when she noticed how many businesses and homes had even a small number of stairs.

The world wasn't built for people like her—the crippled and the incapable. The accident had effectively rendered her unable to participate in society. She would always be on the outside looking in unless someone was kind enough to take pity upon the poor wheelchair-bound woman and help her inside, because she couldn't help herself. She would always be the burden on people's lives. Regardless how much people might genuinely be willing to help, she would not let herself be a burden.

Maggie's course of direction from the library became clear. Instead of turning home, she continued to push herself towards the southern end of town—towards the bridge out of town on Highway 789.

She was tired of the guilt that weighed on her. Not just for being a burden, but the night of the wreck kept playing in her mind. She knew it was the driver's fault in the brown truck. Whoever it was, they had crossed that yellow line and caused Maggie to swerve to avoid collision. But she was certain there was something she could have done. To this day, she wasn't sure what, and that was part of the problem. If she had been better, if she had known more, she would be walking, and Brandon would still be alive. She couldn't blame someone else for her shortcomings any more than she could expect someone to carry her up and down every step she would encounter in life. As much as the driver of the truck was at fault, she was more at fault. She should have been more in control.

Maggie rolled up to the middle of the bridge, a subdued affair stretching across a small river with a hip-high barrier. Her arms burned at the strength she had to fight to get this far.

Not long now, Maggie thought to herself. *Just one little barrier and then no more pain.*

Maggie glanced around. Occasionally, there was a motor in town, or the revving of engines down by the trailer park, but it was otherwise quiet. No one was heading for the bridge. By the time anyone would know something was amiss, it would be over.

She allowed herself a minute to rest her arms and then Maggie gripped the cement barrier separating her from the edge and shifted her weight forward so that her upper torso leaned into it. Little by little, Maggie maneuvered herself onto the barricade and pulled her leg over the side so that it dangled over the river.

Turning, Maggie pulled on her pajama pants to bring her other leg up as well. Her arms were so sore, however, and the grip she had on the barricade slipped. Maggie suddenly lurched towards the river, her hands desperately clutching onto the rough cement corner as her leg also caught on it.

Panic set in as the sound of the river grew louder. A thread of doubt lurched in her stomach, knotting up as she questioned her decision. She could think of nothing other than pitching headfirst into the water and being carried away by a current that could only be navigated by a capable swimmer. Faced with it, in the moment, the thought gave Maggie pause.

No, I made my decision, Maggie thought, steeling her nerves. *I'm not going through another day of this.*

Maggie's fingers grew tired and sore. As much as she wanted to decide precisely when she dropped, having a moment to say some silent goodbyes, she wasn't sure she had that time.

Lost in her own world, Maggie had not seen the truck pull up or anyone step out of it. She only noticed she was no longer alone on the bridge when the driver hopped the barrier and stood on a small ledge on the outside of it.

Maggie strained her neck to see.

"Chelsea?" she asked, confused.

"Hey," Chelsea said, the tone of her voice not acknowledging the situation they found themselves in.

Maggie eyed her student as Chelsea hooked a hand on the barrier and leaned backwards over the water.

"So, whatcha doin'?" Chelsea asked.

"What are you doing here?" Maggie asked.

"You haven't been answerin' the phone, was starting to think somethin' was wrong."

Maggie had spent enough time with Chelsea to spot the slightest curve at the edge of her mouth—the coy, tongue-in-cheek downplaying of the situation.

“Go home, Chels.”

“Nah, can’t do that. I got a math test comin’ up and—”

“I’m tired, Chelsea. I can’t sleep. Every time I close my eyes, I see those headlights. I see Brandon and I…I just can’t take any more.”

“Sounds rough, Mags. So, we doin’ this?”

Maggie rolled her eyes, her breath growing shallow as her muscles ever-so-slowly weakened, threatening her grip on the barrier. “You’re not jumping, Chelsea. You’re not. You’re gonna wake up tomorrow and be fine. But this isn’t going away. Go home.”

“Here’s the way I see it,” Chelsea explained. “You’re giving up. So, why shouldn’t I?”

“Oh, don’t use my words against me. You have no reason to.”

“Neither did you. But you didn’t give up on me.”

Maggie sighed and glanced down into the water below. It wasn’t a rushing river. Truth be told, Chelsea would survive the fall and easily swim to shore. But Maggie didn’t want to risk it. She’d decided to do this because she felt responsible for costing one person their life. Even if this would be her end, she didn’t want another life burdening her soul, and Chelsea deserved better. It’s why Maggie had worked so hard to tutor her.

Maggie’s breaths turned sharp as tears formed at the corners of her eyes.

“I can’t do this on my own,” Maggie said.

“You’re not alone, Mags.”

Chelsea pulled herself back in and shuffled along the bridge until she was between Maggie and the river, and then muscled Maggie up until she was lying along the barrier. Chelsea had always been one of the physically strongest girls that Maggie knew. Still, it surprised Maggie as her friend hopped the barrier, picked Maggie up onto her back and gave her a piggyback ride over to the beat-up, puke-orange truck that belonged to Chelsea’s parents, and deposited Maggie into the passenger seat.

Chelsea got the wheelchair in the back and then hopped into the driver’s seat. She turned the key, bringing the engine and radio to life. As the chorus of “Livin’ on a Prayer” by Bon Jovi filled the cab, Maggie tried to drag herself across the bench seat. Arms failing her, she settled for lying down with her head on Chelsea’s leg, a little more certain she might make it after all.

Colvill Park, 1976

by Renee Gilmore

Renee Gilmore was born in California and grew up in a small town in Minnesota. She identifies as a person with a disability. She received her bachelor's degree from the University of New Mexico, and her master's degree from Hamline University. Her work has appeared or is upcoming in The Raven Review, Peauxdunque Review, *and* Eastern Iowa Review. *She lives in suburban Minneapolis with her husband Steven.*

It's 8:00 AM on a Tuesday morning, in a small Minnesota town, in the summer of freedom. Our parents signed us up weeks ago, both to keep us from drowning in the river, and to keep us from asking *what's there to do* fifty times a day. We gather outside the ancient concrete building, yawning, all bony arms and legs, shag haircuts and red, white, and blue t-shirts, flagging the bicentennial. We file in, boys on one side, girls on the other, and each grab a wire basket off the metal counter to hold our street clothes for the next hour. We change quickly in the locker rooms, our feet already starting to prune on the cold, wet, concrete floor. We try to ignore the bodies around us, naked and awkward, as we maneuver under towels, dump our clothes into our baskets, and poke the large metal safety pin with the basket number into the hip or shoulder of our swimsuits. We dump the baskets back on the counter with a thump, to be shelved by the bored teenage attendants. We dash through the cold showers and insist we are clean.

Whistles blow and lessons commence. We're ordered into the blue sea of a pool—Olympic sized, unheated. We've already learned that easing into the water is the worst idea. We jump in and cling to the rough sides of the pool, dozens of us, like shipwrecked sailors hoping for a miracle. Goosebumps form on our scrawny arms, and the lifeguards shriek their whistles if a swimmer appeared to be drowning (themselves or someone else).

American crawl, sidestroke, and butterfly were our currency. We hoped to earn another Red Cross card by the end of the summer. Fish to Flying Fish. Flying Fish to Shark. Permission to fly off the highest diving board was our gold standard. After an hour of instruction of dubious quality, mostly by hungover college students, a disembodied voice announced over the crackling loudspeaker that our time was up and to leave the pool—no running. We crowded the counter like puppies, to retrieve our baskets of street clothes, damp bodies in towels, jostling and pushing, smelling of chlorine and unbrushed teeth.

Once dressed, wet swimsuits in plastic bags, stringy hair in our eyes, we stampede the snack bar. The kids with money get Snickers bars and ice cream sandwiches, while the rest of us buy banana Laffy Taffy or root beer Popsicles.

We sit at picnic tables or on the matted grass, or walk around the park, comrades-in-arms after the morning's session. We wait for the parade of parents and grandparents in sedans and station wagons, some eager to hear about the morning's lesson, and others, calculating the minutes until they had to be back at work.

We all head home, back to the endless possibilities that only summer vacation can bring. September felt years away, and our only jobs are running through the sprinklers, and orchestrating complicated sleepovers like they are military maneuvers. We talk our dads into grilling hotdogs for dinner, and play kickball until the streetlights came on, our signal that the day has ended, and it is time for bed.

I Don't Love You Anymore
by Kit McBee

Kevin/Kit McBee is a swimming and aerobics instructor living in Holland, Ohio. He has had multiple poems published in The Mill *for the University of Toledo as well as in* Of Rust and Glass. *Though primarily involved with aquatics, Kevin moonlights in the restaurant world and tries to find time for creative pursuits like poetry, song, and dance. Kit is always happy to see his poems receive life through publication, so he would like to thank the editors for their support over the years.*

We're somewhere on the road,
the beater's running out of fumes.
We're circled by an owl of all things.
This is how I dreamed it would happen,
from a pot to a stove to a cold and empty furnace.
The radio's playing a song I have never heard before
about being in love with wrong, who feels the same;
you've fallen asleep-
it hurts my mind to wonder
if I'm doomed to remain
beneath a crowning moon
with you
forever.
I wish I'd worn a better outfit.

corn filled day dreams
by Vanessa Hernandez

Vanessa Hernandez is a Toledo School for the Arts graduate and has studied Creative Writing under Mr. Justin Longacre and Mr. Mark Allred. She has been previously published in the Wingless Dreamer *and has won third place for Ode to the Zipcode in 2021. Vanessa is the assistant director of El Corazon de Mexico Ballet Folklorico. She plans to continue writing poetry while attending the University of Toledo.*

driving in the center of heartland
we will be going past the same
corn field for what seems like an
hour or five, i'll point out the
hurdles of cows and baby horses

we'll stop along the side of a country
road, take off our shoes and enter
the corn, barefoot and not afraid as
fingertips brush against skin like gentle
husks

like a farmer fertilizes the soil for
bountiful harvest, we will become one
with the corn, tangled in the long green
leaves and forgotten weeds, dandelions
invade the four chambers of my heart

we'll return to small towns owned by
the blue collared and circle k gas stations
with workers too tired to get the pop
machines working

inside me will grow children with kernel
colored hair and eyes that stretch
like the Great Lakes, they'll have minds
greater than the high-level bridge and will
learn to find more than just corn stalks
and "you'll do better in Toledo" signs

because as time grows on we'll find
dandelions rooting us into the soft earth,
holding us close, i'll come to find
corn is just corn, but i'll keep corn
children, broken pop machines, and
dandelions in the center of my heartland

In the Mower's Wake

by A.S. Coomer

A.S. Coomer is a writer and musician. Books include Birth of a Monster, Memorabilia, The Fetishists, Shining the Light, The Devil's Gospel, Misdeeds, *and several others. Recordings include* Rural Eminence Volumes I, II, and III, Goddamn it Anyway, Badlands, Old Fort Sessions, Late Nights in Philpot, *and several others. He runs Lost, Long Gone, Forgotten Records, a "record label" for poetry. He coedits Cocklebur Press, a small poetry press for "books that stick." @ascoomer/www.ascoomer.com/www.ascoomer.bandcamp.com*

I see a robot mowing the spaces between headstones at the sprawling cemetery just off New Hartford Road. Though I scan the rows of granite, sparkling like glass shards under the oppressive sun, I see no one with controls. I don't know what I expect, a grave digger with a new toy? A proprietor, wallet fat with COVID profits, trying to weed out the need for a groundskeeper? Or are they humoring their mechanically inclined kid?

From the relative quiet of my pickup, I watch the way the mower glides along the even rows, doing its slow waltz over buried bones. I wonder if it's a danse I could learn. Me and my two left feet, slumped shoulders, and downcast eyes, one-two, one-two, pivot, spin. I hum along with a melody distinct from the jazz coming through the speakers in my doors, but it's off and I stop. This is something slower, not quite a dirge but definitely a funeral march's kissing cousin. Even the grass got in on the action, flitting from the shoot to catch in the slight breeze and fall in graceless clumps that I could appreciate. You can almost hear the chorus of surrender as blades cut blades.

A honk from behind returns my attention to the road. The light changed, and a minivan full of children headed to the dance studio ahead inches closer. I take one last look at the mower gliding across all that green then, reluctantly, pull away. Part of me wants to turn into the parking lot and follow in the mower's wake, a new funeral procession, picking up snatches of its song of leveling. Maybe open my tentative jaws and see if the melody would take root next to crown and filling. But I've never been good at singing the songs of others.

As I drive towards the guitar shop to replace some dead strings, I can't help but notice the weedy yards surrounding the identical, forty-year-old houses—all flecks of peeling white paint and crooked, ripped screen doors banging out a rhythm I can't follow—are yellowed, sunburnt from twenty days without rain. Despite straining ears and rolled down windows, I can't hear anything faintly resembling music now, just a rusted gate grating groan. I could whistle, but what a cliché.

Winter Depression

by Suzanne Zipperer

Suzanne Zipperer has always been a writer between community work, raising children, making a living, being a friend, and all the other excuses she uses to avoid writing. Suzanne lives in northeastern Wisconsin on her family farm. She doesn't farm; it's more work than writing. She has published many pieces of non-fiction, a couple of poems, and several short stories. After quitting for nearly 20 years, Suzanne revisited her novel How We Got Here *and is looking for a publisher.*

The metal click woke me as suddenly as an unchecked alarm clock. I pulled the quilt tighter and glanced at the frost-thick window. There was no seeing out, but from the shaft of bright sunlight trying to break through the feather crystals, I sensed it was just dawn.

Dawn on a January day. Another cold January day. The sun would shine in a clear blue sky for an hour or two, then the wind would pick up, pushing in the greyness. The winter grey. Perhaps a bit of snow, perhaps enough to isolate us for yet another day.

I pulled the wool-filled quilt tighter and curled up into a ball, tucking my knees into the old flannel nightgown. Why was this room always so cold? I could feel the air leaking in through the window of the old farmhouse.

Then it came again—the two fast, hard, metallic clicks. I knew the sound. It was the chamber of the shotgun being opened. First, the bolt pushed up against the top of the barrel. Click. Then it slid back to expose the chamber. Click. Click-click. Click-click. Then came a harder click, the barrel being snapped away from the stock.

I rolled onto my back, letting in some of the cold air to wake my senses. My ears strained for the sounds from the room below. He was never back in the house this early. He had chores to do. But lately after the morning milking, he'd be back in to sleep until early afternoon. Even with the cold, that was very unlike him.

What was he doing? He hadn't even touched his gun during the past hunting season, said he had no interest in walking through the woods, freezing, chasing some silly rabbit. Said his legs were getting too old for even that little bit of sport.

My mind drifted back to the warm May day. The lilacs bloomed along the narrow cemetery road as the line of cars paraded around to halt aside the black hearse. The coffin, the same shade as the lilacs, was pulled slowly from the rear and rested alongside the pile of spring-moistened earth. The sun bounced off the metal handles.

Everything contrasted so sharply. The drab of our dark clothes against the bright green of yet to be clipped grass. The laughter of children playing in the schoolyard cutting through the weeping that surrounded us. The birds singing to their mates as I held tight the trembling hand of my father who was burying his.

Spring, yet the winter depression was in our midst. Bitterly, I thought of how unfair it was that she fought the winter off, only to be taken before the summer brought the sun's healing rays.

I looked down at the hand I held so tightly. Poor Dad. Now should have been the time for them. The last child was gone from the nest. The years of working together were finally paying off. Security, money to spare, time to relax and find each other again.

Thirty-five years of marriage, four kids, a farm mortgage paid, and now he's alone. Thirty-five years in the same bed. Thirty-five years and now the loneliness, at an age when a man shouldn't be lonely.

In the room beneath, I could barely hear the squeak of the cleaning rod being assembled, the three parts twisted into each other. I pictured the black cotton wad being pushed into the barrel and turned as it poked through, loosening any tiny particle which could alter the direction of the bullet.

My mind wandered to the week before.

"Why don't you help me paint the upstairs bedroom?" There was another blizzard. Outside the wind whipped the snow into wicked ghosts ready to place their icy fingers on your face.

"I'm tired." The TV was set to some ridiculous game show as he lay dozing on the couch.

"You sleep too much," I said. "You sleep all the time. Get up and do something."

"But I can't sleep at night," he protested. "Besides, it's too cold out. Ya can't paint when it's so cold. Ya gotta be able to open up the place. You know that."

I knew it was depression that made him sleep, depression and maybe the instinct to hibernate.

I myself was warding off the same. My life had taken an unexpected reverse, and I found myself once again, after seven years, under my father's roof.

"Daddy…" Six weeks ago I stood in the doorway, suitcase in hand. "Dad, I know you'll think this is terrible, but I left Bob, and I have nowhere to go. We're getting a divorce and…" The tears flowed and my planned, calm, brave explanation caught in the current spilling from my brain, out my eyes and down my face.

It was a week later before I was composed enough to talk. But then, as usual, I couldn't find the right words to explain it to him.

"But Dad, you don't understand. It isn't that we didn't try. It just doesn't work. We want two different things. I can't live the way he wants me to. I'm not that kind of a woman. I need more out of life."

"Don't you think you should have thought of that before you got married?" He sat in his usual place at the table, looking down into his cup of coffee as he spoke in his deep, slow voice. "I should have thrown you out the door as soon as you came." He stopped short, as if thinking twice on his words.

"Well, I'll go if you want me to," I said quietly, a lump forming around the words. I knew it was wrong to involve him in our problems. I was childish to run home to Daddy. Mom wouldn't have allowed it. She would have turned me away, but I played the game, played to his loneliness with Christmas and the long winter ahead. I needed to be away from Bob, to have time and space to think of my next move. I was using Dad, and he knew it, but the benefit was mutual.

A heavy silence hung between us. I stood up and went to the stove to get more coffee. Refilling the cups, I thought that all a father expects from his daughter is that she marry and be happy. The son must be a success, even better than the father, but the daughter can slide by with being only a wife. I had failed, even in that small expectation. I had failed him

"I don't know," he broke the silence. "You're married for seven years and a few things go wrong and then just cut him out."

"I didn't just cut him out." I took the coffee to the table and sat down again. "And it wasn't just a little problem. We're arguing constantly." My hands shook as I put the cup to my lips. The steam moistened my eyes.

"Well, your mother and I had problems too," he said. "You kids have it a hell of a lot easier than we did. You have no children. Your own house. Good jobs. We had nothing. Four kids and I was out of work half the time, until we bought this place. Then your ma went to work to help pay for it as well." He never looked up from the coffee. "She took care of the house and helped me outside too. You think she ever had time to herself? You think she ever thought of living her own life? You're damned selfish is all."

I lost control. The tears flowed down, and I remembered all the mornings I lay in bed listening to them arguing downstairs. I remembered the silence at the supper table, the distance, the defeat.

"Yes," I answered. "And that is why she was always so frustrated. She never did anything the way she wanted, and she just became more and more bitter, and her whole life was cheated away." I felt sick. I put my head down on the table and cried. He stood up, walked into the hall, pulled on his overalls, and walked out the door.

Sorry was a word never heard in our house.

***

Click. It came again. The barrel being snapped into place. I held my breath, waiting. Footsteps sounded across the floor and the door of the gun cabinet squeaked open. The footsteps returned to the table. I heard the sound of shells being emptied from the box, rolling out onto the Formica tabletop. What was he doing? Why this ritual so early in the morning?

***

"BRRR. Merry Christmas everybody," Aunt Clara came in stomping the snow off her feet and onto the braided rug at the doorstep.

"Brrr. Christ, when will it end, hey?" Uncle Ed followed behind her. "Either below zero or snowing every day. Merry Christmas everybody."

We had decided to continue the traditional Christmas Eve dinner with Mom's brother and his wife and their family. Everyone was home with their spouses and kids, so the house was full of activity. It made the shortage of the one important parent a little less noticeable. We tried to make the usual dishes, but the rolls didn't turn out like Mom's old recipe card promised.

"How's your dad doing?" Aunt Clara cornered me in the kitchen.

"Oh, fine, I guess. The winter is getting to him. Nothing to do you know. It's easier in the summer when there's plenty of work. He doesn't seem to want to do much of anything."

"Yes, and I suppose he doesn't get out much either with the roads icy and all." She dished the pickles Mom had canned two years before onto a cut glass plate. "We think so often too that we should invite him for dinner or something, but then something always comes up. You know how it is."

"By the way, I haven't seen Bob," Clara looked around the corner and into the living room where the men were seated.

"Oh, uh, he didn't come with me this year," I stammered and turned toward the sink so she couldn't see the flush redden my face.

53

"He decided to have Christmas in Indianapolis with his own folks for a change."

"Oh, yes," Clara said between snitched mouthfuls of food. "I suppose. He's been here every other year. He's OK though?"

"Oh yes. Busy as always." Divorce was still a dirty word in our Roman Catholic family, and I was the first to tread the forbidden path.

The dinner table was alive with chatter. John's new girlfriend had to be filled in with all the family secrets and stories about what a devil he was.

"Good God, no wonder I'm grey." Dad said holding back his laughter behind the usual stoic face. He seemed to be enjoying having us all together, but every once in a while, I'd glance up to see just the slight bit of a quiver around his lips.

Later we sat in the living room with a drink. Greg and Judy had taken the kids home to bed. John and his friend went out for a private drink, leaving only my eldest brother Pete, my aunt and uncle, Dad, and myself.

"So, how's the milk price been?" Uncle Ed asked.

"Oh, all right, I guess, when they can get in to get it. Last week I had to hold it a day. With all the damned snow it's four o'clock before the roads are cleared so the truck can get in to pick it up," Dad answered, looking down into the ashtray where he tapped his cigarette.

"How's your knees holding out?" Aunt Clara joined in with her usual chipper tone.

"Oh, geez, getting old, I guess. Hurts all the time. Arthritis get in the both of them now. Damned cold weather don't help any."

"Yeah, well you'll have to sell the place and move to Arizona." Clara laughed.

"Might as well." He pushed to the edge of the chair and leaned his elbows on his knees, staring down between separated feet. "Kids don't want the place. No use working myself to death."

"You don't think of farming, Pete?" Uncle Ed shifted the attention from my father.

"Can't afford it," Pete answered. "I'm not into doing sixty-hour weeks without overtime either. Price of milk goes up and the machinery goes up three times the amount. No, there's just no future for the small guy anymore."

"Why don't you rent it out and find a little job in town to keep you busy?" Ed redirected the conversation to Dad.

"Yeah, but I'm sixty years old. Nobody wants you then. I could tend bar or something, but that's on your feet all day too." He reached over the coffee table for another cigarette "Can't afford to retire yet."

"No, you couldn't just sit around anyway. That would end you for sure," Clara chirped. It was always said that a farmer could be as healthy as a bull until the day he retired, then drop dead of a heart attack two weeks later.

"Yeah, so it goes when you get old, hey?" Dad stood up. "You want another drink?" he asked and without waiting for a reply walked into the kitchen.

"It's rough alone, hey?" Clara whispered. "Be different if he weren't alone. They could travel or even move away together, but it's harder when he's alone."

The holiday ended too quickly. The house emptied, guests stopped coming, and I felt the acute loneliness that hangs in the house that was once filled with family noises.

The January wind froze us as well. We talked less and less. Television brought the news. Mail came through the snow, but the mood fell with the temperature. I too was sleeping now, getting up only to put the coffee on and crawling back into bed. I felt so alone. There was no one here I could talk to. Everyone who knew the situation was back there, with Bob. I was supposed to be looking for my next job but couldn't even put a resume together. I wanted so bad to talk to Dad, to make him understand, to relieve some of my guilt. But that was impossible. It was then I realized why I married Bob, and why I was divorcing him

***

Click. It came again. The barrel snapped back into place. Click. The chamber bolt snapped up. I heard the cartridges roll together as he fumbled to pick one up and place in the chamber. Click, the bolt snapped back into place.

I lay there. I lay there and listened. Thinking. The depression. The winter depression. For me, the spring would come again. For him? He was so silent the last few days. He didn't sleep but stared out into the blinding snow for hours. Was this it? Was this his choice? His solution? And what of me? Have I the right to interfere when all the while I didn't break the silence and help him? Doesn't he really know what is best for him? What of the others? Will they blame me if I don't stop it?

I heard the front door open. The footsteps crunched loud across the snow. My heart pounded. I dared not breathe less I miss a sound. Then it came.

Shedding Skin
by Amie Tara Brodie

Amie Tara Brodie is a United Methodist minister at a rural church called The Farmhouse in Metamora, OH, which is theologically based in the Agrarian tradition of land care and community. She writes poetry and essays to process what she is learning or thinking about. Much of the focus of her writing centers on her small farm in Oregon, OH named Amie's Acre and the church property in Metamora, along with the people and animals who are part of that community. She is married and has 2 dogs, a mischievous cat, 3 hens and a rooster, a hive of bees, and an old-lady horse. Out at The Farmhouse there are 3 sheep and another hive of bees, as well as an orchard and gardens. They are a varied and lively source of inspiration.

It looked like a spider was clinging to the screen
It stood between my eyes and the view out my window
As I wrote,
Interrupting my placid sentences like an eight-legged asterisk.
Should I look down the page to see what it was noting?
Because it wasn't a spider at all, just a husk;
Not really a statement, just a mark remaining
Maybe to hold the place of what the spider meant to do
When it was halted by its need to change—
Right there—no waiting,

No seeking of a safe place to hide
So that no one could watch, or take advantage
Of its soft vulnerability;
Sharp beaks are always at the ready.

How much better it would be to hide,
Creep into some small space
And come forth transformed, brand new,
No one to remember the chinked and stale armor
That had become weakened
In the onslaught of living,
And begun to split embarrassingly
When it most needed to be strong.

It made me wish for darkened cracks
In basement walls or under bark,
Where I could leave the shell of who I used to be behind;
I'd rather no one see me squirm and writhe
As I peel my layers back; how I flay myself
To rid myself of that old casing,
Inadequate now, not good enough.

I am as much afraid as any spider
To be caught in the open, unprepared
In skin too worn thin
To cover all the holes I feel unraveling.

Elixir of Life
by Cassandra Morgan

Cassandra Morgan is an author, writing coach, and speaker residing in Toledo, Ohio. She writes in several genres, though there is always a little magic in everything she creates. Her works include The Kingdom of Chartile *series,* The Silver Fox Mysteries, *winner of the Cat Writer's Association 2020 Muse Medallion,* Damsel in Social Distance, *and her short story,* "The Witch of Eisenwald Forest," *in the* Dream of Darkness *anthology. She lives with her husband and six su-purr-lative felines, where she thrives on coffee, courage, and kitten cuddles.*

A shaft of light fell across Queen Juliana's face, kissing her cheek with the gentle touch of warmth that only the season of Awakening could bring. She forced her eyes open, glancing out the tower window. The boughs of the trees hung with icy fingers, now beginning a delicate drip in the thaw.

She threw off her bed covers with as much as her strength allowed. Spring may have arrived, but she felt the life slipping from her moment by moment. The looking glass above her vanity revealed the dark circles beneath her eyes, and her skin looked ashen and gray.

In the corner hung the Queen's Spring raiment, the guise of her work laid ready before she set to slumber. It seemed to taunt her as she felt the ache in her bones, like a last touch of Winter's breath still lingered in her joints. If she was to carry out her task, if she was to help usher in the Spring for her kingdom, she needed to feel life within her again. The alchemist would know what to do.

Ignoring the uniform of her profession, Juliana threw open the door to her bed chamber. The hall outside was empty. The doors to her children's rooms disclosed the quiet slumber they still kept within. With sluggish steps, Juliana crept past, making her way down the spiraling stair.

The light of Spring streamed through the windows, welcoming and beckoning her into its arms.

"Not yet," she croaked to herself. "For I am not yet whole and young again." She raised a hand to her cheek, wondering if she looked as dead as she felt.

She smelled her beloved and loyal alchemist's work before she saw him. He stood over the heat, poking and prodding his various concoctions.

"Good morning, my Queen." He turned from his work and lifted her hand to his lips.

"It should be a good morning, dearest one, but I feel my very essence drained from me as I slept. I require the Elixir before I can beset myself to my task."

The alchemist smiled and, kissing her hand once more, turned back to his work.

Juliana knew not his secret for making the Elixir of Life. She had tried it herself, but it never seemed as good as when her dear alchemist made it for her. He measured the little seeds so carefully, crushing them into a fine powder. He used only the purest water from the fountain in the corner, and she wondered if he did not bless it on his way back to his cauldron.

As the Elixir brewed, the alchemist led Juliana to the table by the window and wrapped her in a blanket pulled fresh from the launders.

"You need more than just the Elixir, my love. You cannot go to work without sustenance."

Before she could speak her surrender, a plate of eggs, toast, and fruit appeared before her. She lifted a withered hand to his cheek, her soul proclaiming her appreciation as their eyes held each other.

A gentle trickle of water called the alchemist back, and the Queen watched him work, adding just a few more ingredients and stirring the Elixir as he crossed the room toward her. She reached out, and the alchemist set the steaming concoction into her hands. The warmth radiated through the cup, like the kiss of Spring on her cheek she had felt as she awoke. She lifted the Elixir to her lips and felt the steaming hot potion coat her tongue in splendid, bold flavors, felt the brew trickle down her throat, its effects spreading throughout her body, feeding life into her soul again.

Queen Juliana's eyes remained closed for many more glorious sips, feeling the potion's effect fill every inch of her body, feeling life flood into her again. When she opened her eyes, she smiled at the coy grin her alchemist held upon his face.

"Better, my Queen?" Juliana's husband asked as he leaned against the counter.

"Oh, yes," she said, setting the cup upon the kitchen table.

"Good." He emptied the coffee grounds into the little bowl they used for their compost. "I know you wanted to tackle pruning the south garden today."

Juliana took another deep drink, and rose from the kitchen chair, leaving the dryer-warm blanket behind. She kissed her husband. "I couldn't have done it without you."

A door opened upstairs, and she heard the patter of tiny feet running down the hall to the bathroom.

"That's my cue," he said, pulling out a fresh skillet and readjusting the apron around his waist.

Juliana lifted the coffee cup between her hands, heading for the stairs. She paused, one foot set upon the first step as she turned, looking at her husband as he worked the stove, making the kids Saturday morning breakfast.

"I still don't know how you do it."

He paused from whisking his eggs, just long enough to glance at her. "What's that, my Queen?"

"How do you get this to taste so good?"

That coy grin spread across his lips again. He winked and said, "Magic."

Two Poems
by Michael Kocinski

*Michael Kocinski is an illustrator, poet, and grant writer. He lives in Columbus,
OH with his wife, two sons, and two cats. When he's not working you can find
him creek fishing or reading comics.*

Quickening

At my daughter's cross-country meet
I walk through piles of wind heaped maple leaves
with my son. He's two years old
and the leaves are bigger than his hands.
We drag our feet through them and kick
those scarlet and yellow spanners up
and watch them tumble in the breeze
like these high school runners, almost
light as air as they stream by in their
bright sneakers skidded with mud and
silk jerseys blazing with colorful mascots.

My daughter emerges from the woods
running across the soccer field, approaching
the last leg of the race. She's red faced,
striding out the final yards, she's graceful,
perfect joints greased with sunlight, quiet
and weightless as a gazelle on the savannah.
Her brother calls her name, breaks my grip
on his coat and runs across the chalk lines
defining the course. He wants to run, too,
and merges with the stream of runners
shrinking again in the distance, so many
windblown leaves, on their way to the finish line.

Grackles

I think they must all have been
heavy equipment operators or
veteran farmers in their past lives.
It's the way they walk,

I imagine their lunch-pail swagger,
the iridescent grease and oil stains
on thick cotton work blues,
the metallic sheen of daily blue jeans.

They rolled when they walked
back then, too, favoring distressed
joints and muscles wracked by use.
Still, their eyes did glint and shine

with avian brightness under buzzing
fluorescent tubes and sunlight hung
by chains from the ceiling or sky.

Now they wander lawns, heads cocked,
purple tongues in the garden lapping up
windfall mulberries, glittering insects,
seeds, even bits of stone and metal,

singing their guttural odes in choruses.
No human memory troubles their minds,
you can see it in their eyes, round and
bright as rivets in a pair of bib overalls.

Two Poems
by Michael Brockley

Michael Brockley is a retired school psychologist who lives in Muncie, Indiana where he is looking for a dog to adopt. His poems have appeared in Pine Cone Review, The Parliament Literary Journal, *and* Visiting Bob, Poems Inspired by the Life and Art of Bob Dylan. *Poems are forthcoming in* Borderlines Journal, Last Stanza Poetry Journal, *and* Marrow Magazine.

America, when

a man has lived a long time, he learns the rules of order for debating the sentience of forests in the town square of his narrow, haunted bed. Such a man hoards the novels of tricksters and arranges them by prank and punk. And listens to the music neither of his friends has ever heard. Bhi Bhiman, Mitski, Thao and the Get Down Stay Down. America, you crowd your ghost towns with a menagerie of jacks. Jack-in-a-box, jackalope, jack o'lantern, Jack Daniels, Jack the Ripper, Jack Frost, jackhammer, jack-off, jackknife, jackanapes America, I want a different anthem. I want to root for a championship team where Wonder Woman bats cleanup. This time I want a father. And a slice of drunken nut pie. America, walk through the neighborhoods where your soldiers are grown. Watch them stumble in the home stretch of their relay races and lose their breath before blowing out the candles. Listen to the voices of jaguars and rivers. Listen to someone play an instrument you can't pronounce. Revive Little Richard and beg him to sew a new flag. Change the logo on the stationary. This time let's call ourselves the United States of Mercy.

American Dream, Plan B

The last time you saw her she wore a yellow sundress and introduced you to the man she planned to marry after his residency in the university town that honors Hoagy Carmichael. You ordered lunches from her off a hand-printed menu in a coffee shop with scuffed hardwood floors. Beet salads with cherry tomatoes, shredded carrots, green beans, nicoise olives, and herb goat cheese. She paused between refilling water glasses or sweeping the floor to speculate on the motivations of henchmen. *Hench* she called them. Beefy guys who wore dark t-shirts with a cryptic word or number printed across the chest. *Scorpion. Rumpelstiltskin.* A reversed seven. *When you're in Noirville,* she said, *Never trust the lackeys. Keep the femme fatales dead center in your rearview mirror.* She hummed Tom Petty songs while she worked. "American Girl" while refilling the salt-and-pepper shakers. "You Got Lucky" during those rare afternoons when she drew the dishwashing straw behind the bar. "The Wild One, Forever" at the conclusion of your chats, after you reminded her she resembled the latest woman to exit your one-trick-pony carnival. On those Saturday afternoons in a city famous for its David Letterman mailbox, she gathered scraps of stray sunlight into the fabric of her sundress and pirouetted about the cafe in that graceful waltz petite women draw upon as they occupy themselves with glamorless chores. While she was busy with homecoming patrons or young debutantes shopping for prom dresses, you wrote notes about her henchmen lore in the margins of your coyote poems. Fragments of lyrics from "Crawling Back to You" and "Running Down a Dream." She advised you to want more than what a woman named for a river could deliver. And was fond of saying, *No one visits The Henchmen Hall of Fame.*

Two Stories
by David Sapp

David Sapp, writer, artist, and professor, lives along the southern shore of Lake Erie in North America. A Pushcart *nominee, he was awarded Ohio Arts Council Individual Excellence Grants for poetry and the visual arts. His poems appear widely in the United States, Canada, and the United Kingdom. His publications include articles in the* Journal of Creative Behavior, *chapbooks* Close to Home *and* Two Buddha, *a novel* Flying Over Erie, *and a book of poems and drawings titled* Drawing Nirvana.

Crazy Car Ride

There was this crazy car ride before Mom was carted off: commitment, state hospital, Thorazine, electroshock, in those early days when there was still hope—when we all assumed that the marriage was salvageable like a small screwdriver adjustment to a carburetor. In 1974, when I was fourteen, a novice obsessive-compulsive, just beginning to fathom what disillusionment meant, Watergate somehow intermingled with, responsible for, the erosion of trust, we motored between Hamtramck Street and Moundbuilders Guidance Center on Coshocton Avenue.

(Why "Moundbuilders?" Is it a place of burial? That's grim. We dig a hole before building a mound where the archaeology of emotion is essential. A place of ritual, the Hopewell were known to expand their edifice for fifty minutes each week—payment on a sliding scale expected at the time of the appointment. And when the center got a new building a few years later, it was located on Blackjack Road implying that a good bludgeoning over the head to alter the phrenological landscape just might do the trick.)

This was a time when community mental health centers began popping up across rural America like monasteries, islands of civilization, across medieval chaos. This was the usual route to Big Bear Supermarket, Woolworths, and the burgeoning fast-food stops. We passed the little shop where we bought our parakeets. With the current errand at hand, this familiarity was turned on end. I was mistaken in thinking we would stop for ice cream after the session.

It was Mom, both grandmothers and I ensconced within the maroon 1970 Ford Galaxy 500. (Where was Dad? My little sister?)

Why we all rode together I could never comprehend. Madness, the error evident when the car was put in gear. To this day I do not know who drove, as if the car moved on its own accord, a sign of the precarious nature of the journey. My memory remains troubled over the gap, rehearsing the logistics again and again. In this closed, black-vinyled space, Mom attempted the word "bastard" in a tangential experiment. Grandma Sapp replied sharply, "We won't have any of that!" Grandma Dearman looked out the window. The idealism of childhood fell away, irrevocably misplaced that day.

These three women became three facets, a trinity, of my personality. Mom was darkly, absurdly hilarious, manic, and dangerously paranoid. She was unquestionably crazy and not in a quaint way. Dorothy Snow, Mom's mom, was irretrievably lost, house-bound, probably abused by her husband—at the very least, emotionally neglected. Each day was a weighty, cumulative burden. She was a silent, invisible tragedy who rarely smiled or knew what love was.

Helen Louise, Dad's mother, was who I worshipped (more than the Eucharist at Sunday mass—happily risking Catholic blasphemy). A practical, forthright matriarch who ruled her husband, the farm, and any kitchen she entered—who sought out and discovered a bit of humor in any situation—except maybe this one, she cried "bullshit" and laughed with equal enthusiasm. And she considered counseling a useless extravagance. (We won't mention her little green nerve pills—likely Valium—stowed in her kitchen cupboard.)

I don't recall my conversation with the therapist or the return trip. The disaster irreparable by then, I don't recall feeling any different or any better. There was a vague futility, though, as if the more pertinent questions were never broached. This therapist was later pressed by lawyers and judges to testify. All three women are long gone now—maybe the therapist as well. I'd like to think I'm the only one driving.

I Should Have Been in Love

When we were five and six, we played with Barbie's dolls on her bed all day on rainy days. Though I don't recall the scripts or scenarios, we explored the roles of adults by assigning our perfect, sexless little people with voices and dramas. Her bed seemed to be the safest place on earth, warm, heavy with her sleep. The stairs, front door, porch, and her mother Margie in the kitchen, a sentinel, a fierce lioness, were between us and our looming ogres. We were still too innocent to comprehend our terror, the intentions of our separate and secretive predators.

When our three families camped along the banks of the Mohican River, when the boys, Tim, Boomer, Doug, and I, disappeared hiking or tubing on our own, Barbie, the only girl, remained behind near the fire. One Halloween the oldest boy, Tim Wheeler, was caught at the throat by a clothesline while running through an old neighbor's backyard. Decades later I remembered the event and imagined, decades before, Barbie surreptitiously smiling at this news – but also wondering why his head couldn't be conveniently and fittingly snapped off like a French aristocrat.

A decade later, when we were fifteen and sixteen, the dolls set aside, Barbie showed me her pet mice. Unlike most girls, she was unafraid of creatures that slithered and scurried. Presiding over their small world, she tended her tiny white and pink wards judiciously and tenderly. She wore baggy jeans, frayed at the hems, and unflattering men's plaid flannel shirts, a costume meant as camouflage to boys' attentions. We rarely saw one-another in the hallways, but she found time to patiently and expertly explain the high school social landscape of jocks, nerds, freaks, geeks, and loners as if hypersensitive to who may be a potential ally or threat. An accomplished loner, I struggled to comprehend the hierarchy or qualifications of my role.

At twenty-five and twenty-six, we said hello too awkwardly in the drugstore downtown where I was ashamed to be found stocking shelves, cosmetics, shampoo, paper products, and pain killers, after dropping out of art school. Her eyes were still soft, kind, and dark; her hair shimmered under florescent lights. Now Barb, not Barbie, she was beautiful, and I should have been in love with her all along. A fleeting, electric moment, a wisdom, passed between us. We could have been co-conspirators in and swapped harrowing tales and strategies of survival.

And four decades later, our lives played out upon separate paths, in a chance phone call, the easy familiarity of those rainy days in our voices, I heard her declare the fact aloud. I learned that she was Tim Wheeler's victim. Somehow, unlike Barbie and the other boys, I was not. My monster came for me from an entirely different tangent. I think I said, "I never would have guessed."

Mine

by Aubrey Brant

Aubrey Brant is a senior at Toledo School for the Arts. She aspires to be a writer of fictional novels, though she is content to create poems and short stories for now. Aubrey enjoys reading, running, and listening to (oftentimes angsty) music. She has lived in Ohio all her life.

In the quiet of night
I finally feel like this town is mine
Nobody's around to say otherwise
And maybe that's why I want it

In the afternoon
The sun claims it
Lighting up anti-abortion signs
And pedestrians that
Might wave back
I wouldn't dare call it mine
Wouldn't even admit I'm part of it

In the quiet of night
Guilt's pounding heartbeat of 4 AM pushing me out
I'm proud to call it mine
Because it's *only* mine

In and around every cul-de-sac
Porch lights gently waving by

Past the corners of the blocks
Backtracking when road meets farmland
Letting shorn cornfields rest

Breezing by fenced-in backyards
Where dogs would bark in the daytime

Avoiding traffic lights
That might have cameras
Not doing anything bad
But still afraid to get caught

For eight miles
It was all mine

In the afternoon
I hold my head so high
I'm out of reception
And it's crowded
And there's no room for me
And I never wanted to be here anyway

But in the quiet of night
That one night
This town was mine

Remember This Face

by Theresa Panuski

Theresa is a born and raised Midwest writer, starting out in St. Louis, going to school in Cape Girardeau, and finally settling in Chicago, after a brief stay on the east coast. Formerly an acquisitions and managing production editor for a small non-profit press, she is currently the full-time caregiver for her two children and a part-time writer and editor. She's been previously published in Death Head Grin, Twisted Tongue, Yellow Mama, *and the online anthology of* Best American Short Stories.

My mother grew up in that season of Catholicism where she was forbidden to wear tampons until after her wedding night. Vatican II changed a lot of things, but the oral tradition that tampons could steal your daughter's virginity wasn't one of them. I, a child of the revolutionary 1990s, was allowed to wear tampons in high school. This was considered a great leniency. But that leniency was bookended by moral righteousness and guilt. This small bending of the rules was not a sign the Church was wrong but that I, a child of modern feminism growing up in the 21st century, was weaker than my foremothers. Concessions were made. But the wearing of tampons did not give me license to engage in "other" sexual activities—as though the tampon was a gateway drug leading to a vibrator, or S/m, or personal ownership of my sexuality.

What my mother couldn't control with her panicked zealotry, the Church controlled with a weapon tempered in the fiery pit of legalized abortion and birth control and the social acceptance of spectrum sexuality. Fear of breaking a part of yourself you don't understand only lasts until you learn or until you engage in the Church accepted ritual of having it taken by your divinely appointed spouse. Fear doesn't last forever.

Shame is a more effective weapon. Shame can survive the most detailed of anatomy classes. You can carry shame with you into the most gentle and consensual of relationships. Shame can follow you down the aisle and into your marriage bed and all the way to your diamond anniversary.

Shame has no expiration date, and the foundation can be laid early.

The transition was subtle and all at once. As I prepared for my confirmation and becoming an adult in the Church, the Jesus of my childhood faded into myth like Santa. This new Jesus spoke with the male voice of the Magisterium and no longer healed the sick or cared for the disenfranchised. This new Jesus did not call me to love unconditionally or act without judgment or show mercy. Now that I was becoming a woman, Jesus had a new message. Jesus, I was told, wanted me to know I was on my way to becoming a half-eaten box of Oreos, a present someone else had unwrapped, and a piece of packing tape someone had used to clean a dirty carpet.

What do all those things have in common?

They're trash.

***

Mrs. K taught me my first lesson on chastity.

After burning out as a corporate executive she'd reverted to the comfort and familiarity of her childhood faith with a fire of passion that didn't so much spark faith in others as it burned, wholesale, anything that was between her and God. This was the unforgiving fire she brought with her into the eighth-grade classroom in lieu of teaching credentials or religious education.

She was a hard woman, big-boned with layers of muscle turned to fat after decades of sitting behind a desk and short brown hair that fluffed around her head like the halo she thought she deserved. She would pace around our classroom in starched khakis that bristled with static electricity, always walking behind us so we never knew quite where she was. When she stopped behind you, you couldn't help but wince, expecting a shock.

Mrs. K never wore makeup and was exacting in her enforcement of the school dress code. Where other teachers would let colored Chapstick or clear lip gloss slide, Mrs. K would make you wipe it off, stopping class until you were "prepared to learn." Vanity was a deadly sin. It had to be crushed underfoot.

Children, young people as she called us, were Mrs. K's least favorite thing and her classes were structured to exterminate what was left of our youth. Her lessons were dull. She read straight from the textbook and made us spend hours copying vocabulary words and definitions in longhand. She used the multiple-choice tests from the back of the teacher's edition and crossed out the essay questions. There was no room for subjective thinking or critical debate in religion. The Word was Law and she was its martial.

The day of our first chastity lesson was the only day of eighth grade I remember Mrs. K smiling.

She came to class late—another once in eighth-grade event—carrying a rectangular box wrapped in white paper and tied with gold, silver, and pearlescent ribbons that merged at the center to form a bow of scissor edged curls. She held the package with a delicacy I didn't think her red, swollen joints were capable of and then set it down on the desk of the class Queen Bee with a reverence she normally reserved for the Body of Christ on Wednesday all-school Masses. I don't remember the girl's name, but at the time it had been seared into my heart with the pain of not belonging. What I do remember is that she was 13 and handling her awkward transition into adulthood with a grace that made me hate her and grown women envy her.

Mrs. K led her into the center of the room, a hand resting at the center of her back.

"Now, choose one of the gentlemen to give the present to."

The girl handed it to the boy closest to her without making eye contact and then turned to retreat to her desk. But Mrs. K's hand was still firm on her back. "Not yet. Don't you want to watch him open it? That's the best part of giving a gift."

We all waited. No one knew where to look.

The boy started at one of the seams, carefully peeling off the tape in an attempt to stretch out whatever this was long enough to get us through to lunch.

"No. No." Mrs. K shook her head and lumbered over. "Rip it. Tear it. Really go at it. You want to see what's inside, don't you?" She illustrated what she meant by grabbing the package and ripping off a chunk of paper, letting it fall to the floor.

The boy acquiesced and ripped off the rest of the paper. Pieces floated down to the floor.

"Now," Mrs. K turned to the girl, "rewrap it and give it to another gentleman."

Mrs. K's voice was hard, her smile cold, her eyes cruel. This was the turning point. The bottom dropped out of the classroom. We were chilled and too young to know what to do. No one had taught us. The girl reached for the tape Mrs. K kept on her desk.

"No!" Mrs. K yelled. "You can only use what you were given."

The girl nodded. She tried to piece the paper back together. She did better than most people could've done.

"Now, you open it." Mrs. K grabbed the present out of her hands and gave it to the next boy, too eager to let the girl do it herself.

He looked pale.

"Rip it, really unwrap it." Mrs. K goaded.

"Um," the boy looked around, searching for another adult who could explain, who could stop it from happening. But we were alone.

"What about you," Mrs. K grabbed the present and moved down the line of boys. "Do you want this present now?"

The boy shrugged, "I guess? What's in it?" He wasn't sure what answer she wanted to hear.

"Of course not." Mrs. K smirked. Now, Mrs. K brought the present back to the girl. "Let's say you're on your way to a birthday party and you've let three other people open a present that was meant for the birthday boy. Would you be ashamed to show up with this mess?"

The girl nodded. She was crying.

"Can you put it back the way it was?"

The girl shook her head.

"Try." Mrs. K's eyes shown, cruelty magnified. She was enjoying this in a way we'd never seen her enjoy a lesson before.

She let it go beyond making a point. The popular girl was in tears on her hands and knees picking up scraps of her dignity while the rest of us looked on, embarrassed for her but silent—glad it wasn't us.

Finally, a boy raised his hand, "Isn't it what's on the inside that counts? I'd take a present even if it was unwrapped." He smiled, proud of himself for uncovering the secret of the lesson.

Mrs. K told him to shut-up.

"I can't do it," the girl said through tears. Surrender.

"That's right. You can't." Mrs. K smirked. "And that's what you'll become if you have sex outside of marriage. Would any of you want to receive her gift now that it's been opened and shredded and given to all these other people?"

We wanted it to be over, so we shook our heads.

"Now remember this. When you're in the throes of passion and ready to throw away your virtue, remember this face." She pointed to herself with her cold smile and cruel eyes. "Remember this face."

***

How far is too far. This next lesson in chastity came courtesy of an engaged couple hired by my all-girls high school to psyche us up about saying no to sex until our wedding night. The couple was young. They'd met in college and recently graduated, working to pay off their debt and pay for their wedding by preaching the Gospel of "not yet." Chastity had worked out for them—so well they'd turned it into a full-time career.

Even before their presentation started, we were required to fill out virginity pledge cards. *I solemnly swear to live a life of chastity waiting for my future spouse.* We were told to keep them in our wallets until our wedding day. Then we would hand them over to our husbands, the new guardians of our virtue.

Their presentation was physical, all wireless mics and running up to the edge of the stage as they delivered another "truth bomb"— a phrase of choice among youth ministers who thought they could preach fire and brimstone in teenage vernacular. Having sex outside of marriage leads to depression! Having sex once makes it harder for you to say no to the next person who asks! Contraception changes your biological makeup and will cause you to be more attracted to bad people! Disease! Abortion! An hour into their presentation they were just throwing out keywords. If the facts don't work for you, ignore them. Or change them.

They made sex sound awful. Wait for marriage? Why have it at all?

Then they wound up for the finale. The woman stepped back, dabbing at the makeup she was sweating off with a tissue, silently yielding the floor to her fiancé. It was only right the guardian of her virtue be given center stage. The man stepped forward, sweat dripping into his eyes and plastering his hair to his head. He fanned himself with his shirt collar and in those seconds he was silent.

I couldn't help thinking the real test of their relationship would be what happened after the speaking engagements and book deals dried up. This was a man, shortish, fattish, and unremarkable, who would struggle to give up the spotlight and the soapbox.

"Now," he started again, bouncing back and forth between sides of the stage. "The question I'm always asked at high schools is how far is too far. What can I do before crossing the line and being unchaste? Let me give you an example. If I'm alone in a room with my fiancé here. She's beautiful. And if I know that being alone with her might lead to sin, then going too far with her is allowing myself to be alone in a room with her.

"Think of it this way." Even from a distance you could tell he loved answering this question. That's why he hadn't given us the chance to ask it. "If you're asked out by a guy and you know he has terrible intentions, should you say yes? Is saying yes to a date, in that instance, going too far? Is leaving with him in his car going too far?

"I would say YES!" He shouts at us, pumping his fist in the air. "Putting yourself in a situation that has the potential to lead to sin is going too far. Say it with me!"

I found myself yelling along not because it made sense but because the current was too strong, and I couldn't find my footing. What happened to being the guardians of virtue? If we said yes to a date, to a dinner, to a kiss, were we really not allowed to say no later? Weren't we allowed to walk away from a boy who couldn't act like a man after we'd given him a chance?

Saying yes wasn't like being baptized. It wasn't one yes for all time.

Was it?

***

After thirteen years of chastity programming, it's hard to have relationships with partners who were raised speaking a different language. Likes, dislikes, consent, hard limits, adventure, safety, birth control, choice...

The only word I could contribute to the conversation was no.

But this no was applauded and reinforced by the women of my parish. I was held up as an example in comparison to others' who'd left the faith or found a way to turn the no we learned into a conversation where they discovered other words that could better express what they wanted to say. They traded their no's for experiences, life, and lessons learned. I wasn't standing firm, I was paralyzed, unprepared for submersion in the world. I had been caged by no's for so long I couldn't survive without them.

I let these women put their arms around me, introduce me to their sons—good Catholic boys who all looked alike—and subsume me into their world. I was quiet. I behaved. And when they put their arms around me and pulled me close, I let my body go as stiff as my smile, pretending that this life was the one I'd always wanted.

I hated every boy I had ever gone on a date with.

That was the part the women of the parish cared about the least.

***

The boy who taught me my last lesson on chastity was named John.

John was one of my mother's good Catholic boys, the kind of Catholic boy that showed up to Protestant Bible studies uninvited with a copy of the Latin Vulgate and an attitude. When asked what he did for a living, he said he was still discerning God's plan for his life after three months in seminary.

I met John at a Theology on Tap event I'd been encouraged to go to as a way to meet like-minded young adults. I was entering that awkward stage of faith where I wasn't sure I wanted to have it anymore. I'd come to this phase later than most, after two decades of existing in a world where there was only faith or desolation, and my

76

mother was digging her nails in, clawing tighter the more I pulled away. I would not be lost. I would be set-up. John was the good Catholic boy who was going to keep me in the Church.

John wore black slacks and a black polo shirt with no logo, badge, or nametag. It reminded me of a priest's clerical black without the collar. I wondered if that was the impression he wanted to give—starched, buttoned-up, and closer to God than me in my pencil skirt and kitten heels. I'd come straight from work. He'd come straight from confession. His hair was as black as his outfit, his skin pale, his face pockmarked and red, constellations of dead stars from forehead to chin.

We sat at a high-top table near the bar, and I stared at the bubbles in my room temperature microbrew while John talked about himself.

"I used to work as a car mechanic. Changing tires and stuff at Walmart auto."

I nodded into my beer, took another drink, anything to avoid eye contact.

"We definitely never talked about religious shit there." He laughed at his own attempt at a joke.

"Is that what you do now?" I made the effort. For my mother. I looked at his hands—pale and spotless. No telltale grime or oil stains or calluses.

"Nah. I'm thinking of becoming a priest. I really feel called to the seminary."

"Oh." I nodded again and took another drink, relieved this set-up was doomed.

"I tried to be a diocesan priest, but they wouldn't accept me into the seminary. Said I talked too much about getting married, having kids. That I should explore a call to married life before making a decision."

I nodded again. Dating a guy "discerning the seminary" is the Catholic equivalent of dating a guy who isn't ready to tell his parents he's gay. This time I drained my glass.

Applause started up around us and the speaker, who we'd only nominally been listening to, went back to his table.

I stood up, a natural endpoint. "Nice to meet you." I smiled and walked over to the bar to close out my tab.

John followed me. "I get the feeling you haven't spent that much time discerning your path in life. Work in an office? Just got a job right after college?"

I nodded, waiting for the bartender to notice me.

"I have to ask, because I ask everyone," John went on.

I waved at the bartender. I'd only had the one drink. I should've paid cash.

"When's the last time you went to confession?"

"Um." I felt like I was talking to my mother. "I don't really believe in confession," I blurted out, hoping the lack of orthodoxy would get him to write me off. "Just not there in my faith yet, I guess." I added automatically because I always do when talking with Catholics who are Catholic by choice and not out of some unresolved, guilt-ridden desire not to disappoint a parent—Catholics who I think are somehow better than me.

"Oh." John gave me an appraising once over as the bartender finally came over with my credit card.

John followed me out to my car even though I'd given no indication I wanted to continue talking to him. In fact, I'd left so quickly he'd had to jog to catch up. He stole the keys out of my hand and stood between me and my car, teasing me about whether or not he should let me drive home even though we'd just met, and I'd nursed one beer the whole night.

He told me I could have my keys back if I gave him my number— so he could text me later and make sure I'd made it home safely.

My brain told me he's a creep and that I should use my pepper spray, walk back into the bar, and call the cops.

My mother's voice told me I shouldn't think things like that about good Catholic boys. My hesitation was just the devil trying to push me away from my faith.

I gave him my number.

My pepper spray was on the keychain with my car keys anyway.

***

John was better in text than in person. So much better he made me forget how uncomfortable I'd been with him in person. He texted every day and called every night. We talked about my work. We talked about faith. He talked about his short-lived time in the seminary and told me he was so grateful we'd met. That there weren't a lot of people in his life he could talk like this with.

I believed him.

He asked if he could come over to my apartment sometime. He'd make dinner. We could talk in person.

I said yes. After all, he was a good Catholic boy. He could be trusted.

***

He walks in with a brown paper bag filled with groceries and heads straight to the kitchen. He doesn't give me a hug hello, he doesn't say anything. He opens every cabinet door. He inspects the contents of my fridge. He passes judgment on my spice rack. He makes my skin crawl.

But he's a good Catholic boy. We'd been taught to believe the same thing. I could trust him because he's the only kind of boy I could trust. I do not ask him to leave even as he walks down the hall that connects my kitchen to the apartment's one bedroom.

"Didn't you promise me dinner?" I laugh, try to turn it into a joke to mask how uncomfortable I'm becoming. Everything is telling me to run. Run. Run.

But it's my apartment. Where would I go? I don't want to leave him here. I don't want to turn my back on him. I don't want my mother to say I haven't given him a chance.

I stand my ground in the hallway. I keep my awkward smile straining across my lips.

I do not say no.

And that's as good as a yes.

Or so I've been taught.

He is gentle when he takes my hand and I follow him into my room, stiff but on my own feet. He tugs at the dress I'd chosen so carefully. Maroon with flowers. It goes past my knees. It's a church dress. A Sunday dress. I try not to cry. I wish I'd worn something I hated. I'd never be able to look at my favorite dress again without remembering his aftershave and his breath and his heat and the way I don't fight when he pushes me on my back.

He starts by looking at me, inspecting me with the same intense focus he used to condemn my spice rack. I close my eyes and focus on my breath so I won't have to focus on the feel of his hands, damning and cruel. Maybe this will be it. Maybe this is enough. He will leave and I can lock the door and be alone with my humiliation.

But no number of measured breaths or thoughts or prayers can mask the sound of his belt buckle, a cheap, reversible black and brown belt that goes with his ridiculous black dress pants that he wears by choice because he doesn't have a job and he could've worn jeans like a normal person, but he doesn't.

There is one last, probing search for a virginity I only learn later isn't a real, physical thing. Not at all like a present or a piece of tape or a box of fucking cookies.

I don't know what he finds, but I find my voice.

No.

Stop.

I try to move away, but he's heavy. He's positioned just right. He holds me down. And then he laughs.

"Give me one, good reason," he whispers in my ear the way another boy might have whispered "I love you."

I close my eyes, but instead of a reason, I find the face of my eighth-grade religion teacher. I had said yes by letting him in the door. I had let things go too far. There is no power left for my no.

You can't re-stick tape.

You can't un-eat cookies.

You can't re-wrap a present you've given away.

When he's finished, he goes into my kitchen, opens my cabinets, and starts to cook dinner.

Michigan Night
by Stephanie L. Johnson

Stephanie Johnson has spent most of her adult life overseas teaching English literature, ESL and Spanish at universities and adult education settings around the world. Her writing usually focuses on the slightly uncomfortable space of the expatriation/ repatriation experience. She has most recently been published in Authora Australis *and* force/fields, *an anthology published by Perennial Press. She is an associate editor at Novel Slices. She is a judge for NYC Midnight. While she is originally from Toledo, Ohio, USA, she is currently based in Sydney, Australia.*

Out in the black cold of a Michigan
winter night, stargazing -
1976.
A Stanley Thermos, warm,
between my kindergarten hands.

A satellite!

Such a rare spotting above frosted empty fields.
Traveling across the void, unmanned,
The closest thing we knew to science fiction
Was fact before our eyes.
We turned from constellations and paused in reverence as it traversed
Our patch of sky.
Punchcard fueled, precarious in its perch above us,
We watched it while it was watching us

Whereupon Acteon Witnesses Artemis Bathing and is Torn Apart by His Own Hands

by Jason Ryberg

Jason Ryberg is the author of fifteen books of poetry, six screenplays, a few short stories, a box full of folders, notebooks and scraps of paper that could one day be (loosely) construed as a novel, and a couple of angry letters to various magazine and newspaper editors. He is currently an artist-in-residence at both The Prospero Institute of Disquieted P/o/e/t/i/c/s and the Osage Arts Community. He is an editor and designer at Spartan Books. His latest collection of poems is The Great American Pyramid Scheme *(co-authored with W.E. Leathem, Tim Tarkelly and Mack Thorn, OAC Books, 2022). He lives part-time in Kansas City, MO with a rooster named Little Red and a billygoat named Giuseppe and part-time somewhere in the Ozarks, near the Gasconade River, where there are also many strange and wonderful woodland critters.*

I would never have thought my own
        personal Gordian knot of psycho-

sexual pathology (which would, later
        in life become so unwound and hopelessly

disassembled, much like an industrial /
        econo-sized can of silly string, one can

imagine, having reached its own maximum
        density point of *pressurized content*) would

turn out to be anchored in the straining knot
        barely holding the comparatively pressurized

contents of my sun-bathing neighbor's
        string bikini together that one summer

when I was maybe 13 and she at least 16
        (but going on 24) and she noticed me

standing there in her backyard where
        I had here-to-fore been pulling weeds

for her mother but now stood frozen
        and fixated upon what was really little

more than dental floss tied in a bow-tie
        knot, whereupon she said "pull it"

which of course I did not, so she did
        and laughed – the moment, one can

imagine, like suddenly being exposed
        to processed uranium, burning itself

forever into the endlessly looping
        video tape of my dreams.

Two Poems
by Jacob Reisinger

Jacob Reisinger is a poet and United States veteran who served for the past 9 years. His service has been in both Active Duty Army and the Ohio Air Force National Guard. He received his creative writing degree from the University of Toledo. Reisinger's work is published and/or forthcoming in Of Rust and Glass, *Southeast Missouri State University Press, and the* Albion Review. *He is currently completing a collection of poems titled,* Blind Eyes that See. *Most of Jacob's work surrounds the story of his service and the lineage of veterans that came before him.*

National Training Center

Our 1068 was packed with green cots,
Green radios, green rucksacks, green helmets-
Buoys of green in colorless sea of gear.

Before I left for the field
Cadre briefed Alpha battery and HQ:
every rotation, somebody dies here.

A week later, a single grain soldier
Was compressed so quickly by truck tires
He turned into glass memory.
His life a memory buried in the desert's forgotten grain cemetery.

We drifted like tumbleweeds toward
The ocean of sand.
I sat in my gunner's swing thinking.

About the kid with a broken leg
Hobbling around on crutches
Cleaning dirty bathroom mirrors.

How they dragged him and a handful
Of other broken bodies here because, like our motto,
Can and *Will.*

Our convoy was short,
We arrived somewhere only coordinates could name.

Later I would throw my body into evening sand
Next to specialists Johns and Bulger.
Our bodies were books in a little free library

Our spines ripe with abuse and careless whims.
We smelt like the ancient mold of sour pages
Mixed with menthol aftertaste.

Bulger told us about the 7th day in the field,
His birthday, gifted him ringworm and
A Pop-Tart cake lit with cigarette candles.

We howled like the desert wolves
Who would soon roam this wasteland
And horrify moonlight squatted soldiers.

A Mirage of Runway Lines
Dedicated to Nour and Samar

Samar's hands construct,
In sign language, a cross.
As the plane takes off
Her left hand engulfs our shared arm rest.

Her hair's purple hue
Only seen in Qatar's December sunrise.
Her home before coming
To America.

Her daughter Nour,
Defined with large sand dune dimples,
Concealed by white mask,
Etched Ford blue ink.

We talk about art, school,
Nour's MCAT exam, my poetry, their lives.
Our words drifting in the glimmer
Between clouds and sun seat.

They were warm like rays
Through airplane windows.
Sweet Like Samar's shared Maamoul dates.

I wondered where their words and smiles were
Amongst the pre-deployment briefs?

I flip through my mental rolodex;
My hands turn card stock labeled
"Political climate of Qatar,"
"Off base threats,"
"Don't pet local animals because rabies,"
"A senior NCO saying we put warheads on foreheads."

The only space I could find was between
The words a veteran asked Nour,
Are you really from Qatar?

I regress into silence.
His question a desert rose
Planted in Al Udeid.
Its pink poise now defined by its razor memories.

It's been a few months
Since our Colorado flight.
I realize I couldn't grant
The mother who fed me,
Daughter who enlightened me,
the courtesy of pronouncing their names.

They tell me its,
Nour like lure with a N,
Samar like summer.

Eddie and Izzy (an excerpt)
by Gary Rabuzzi

Gary Rabuzzi lives in Northeastern Ohio, amid a teetering stack of books. This excerpt is from his sixth book, entitled Who's Got the Action. *His books are available on Amazon.*

Eddie thought about the way he and Izzy met. He was just back from the war and in a bad way; shell-shocked. Nightmares, shaking hands, the whole nine yards. He had no family left, no roots. And he couldn't sit still. So, he didn't. He packed a bag and left his apartment door hanging open. From there, he kept it moving, always. He couldn't stand the quiet. The things he heard in it.

One night, he ducked into a small cocktail bar in downtown Cleveland. He was fresh off the bus. The smoke hung inside the cramped little dive like fog on a country road. The clientele was blue-collar guys with bulging exposed forearms, drinking boilermakers and arguing over bowls of stale peanuts. The jukebox played quiet music loudly. And leaning on it was Izzy.

Christ. She was no bigger than a minute, closer to forty-five seconds. She was blonde, dressed in a lavender number that clung to her body like someone had sewn her into it, the lucky bastard. There were black stockings and probably some other stuff, but he was having trouble taking it all in at once. Later, of course, he would find that he remembered it all just fine. His brain had photographed every last detail and stored the pictures for future reference.

But right then, all he could see was her eyebrows. Some guys were leg men, some guys went for the more intimate parts, but Eddie was a sucker for a dame with interesting eyebrows. They usually denoted a certain sardonic worldview that Eddie found irresistible. She had 'em, all right. Delicate, and arched towards the ceiling, like she was in on a joke. She turned towards him, giving him her profile. It was every bit as delicate and meticulously sculpted as her eyebrows. She took a drag, and a sensual wave of blue smoke drifted out from her mouth, rushing directly up her tiny nostrils. The crimson stain she left on her cigarette was like blood on a dead man's pocket handkerchief.

She was murder.

This dame was like a Christian in a lion's den in this joint. And yet, here she was. Alone in a smoky hole in the wall, surrounded by two dozen lugs that would gladly bite a pool cue in half just to smell her hair. But like the Christian, she walked among them unscathed. There were plenty of eyes on her, but no hands. Not yet.

Eddie stepped to the bar and ordered a boilermaker. Actually, he ordered an old fashioned, but the bartender served him a boilermaker anyway. And he did it without much panache.

"When in Rome," Eddie said to himself. He counted to six before he picked the beer up off the sticky bar and knocked back the gasoline. A shudder wracked his spine.

He turned around and leaned on the bar, scanning the room for the girl. He found her at a table along the far wall, with a guy in a sailor suit. He had jug handle ears and wore his cute little sailor's cap perched high on his head.

Eddie looked at the bar. That was that. He had waited too long. A dame like that was like a foul ball. Everybody dove for her at once. He took another drink of Rheingold and tried to look anywhere else in the room. Sailor bait or not, just looking at her, just knowing someone like that existed out in the world, was enough to put him in a good mood.

Then, he saw her point towards the door, her cigarette between her fingers. The swabbie turned to look, and the girl slipped a buck out of the pile of singles he had on the table. It was so smooth Eddie wasn't sure he even saw it. The cash was in her clutch in one deft movement. Eddie blinked. The beer stopped halfway to his mouth. She was on the grift.

The girl locked eyes with him and froze. She was busted cold. She sent him a plea with her eyes, and he nodded slightly. He turned his back on her and took another sip. It was none of his concern if some sea donkey got jobbed. He was just trying to have a quiet drink.

Another boilermaker landed in his gut on top of the first one, which had itself landed on the pint of paint thinner he smuggled onto the bus in Toledo. He was feeling more or less convivial and engaged the bartender in a rather lengthy and heartfelt (and one-sided) conversation about the Dodgers. He wanted to forget about the dame, but he could feel her eyeballing him from the sailor's table.

After a bit, the sailor excused himself to pump the bilge and the girl stood up and crossed the room. She put the touch on Eddie's elbow, and he turned. He looked at her, then at the hallway that led to the bathrooms, then back at her again.

"You're juggling hot coals, sister," Eddie smiled. "Even a dumb swabbie like Jughead there is gonna tumble to your play sooner than later. You're pushing it."

She smiled nervously and glanced over her shoulder. When she turned back around, her lips were close to his ear, breathing warmth on his neck. "Take me home?"

Eddie tried to laugh. The sound was too loud, though, and too dry. "Listen, kid, if I was in the market to die tonight, you'd be a hell of a way to go."

"You haven't said no," she said.

"You got me there," Eddie said.

She took the third boilermaker off the bar and tossed it down the hatch. "Well, you'd better figure it out quick, handsome, before Rusty gets back from the toilets."

Eddie grabbed his hat.

Of House and Homes (an essay)
by Jamie Wagman

Jamie Wagman is an Associate Professor of History and Gender & Women's Studies and Chair of the Gender & Women's Studies Department at Saint Mary's College in Notre Dame, Indiana. She has a Ph.D. in American Studies and a Gender Studies graduate certificate from Saint Louis University, and an M.A. in Writing from The Johns Hopkins University. Her creative work has also appeared in Burningword Literary Journal, *The Mom Egg Review's* MER VOX, Newfound, *and* The Adirondack Review, *among other places.*

The women in my family have long lied about their ages, names, health, marriages, love, births, and deaths. Sometimes this was self-preservation; sometimes it was merely lying to oneself or the tsking neighbors, the PTA, the receptionist at the doctor's office. We all think we have an audience when most often, no one is watching. People are all too busy pulling down the blinds over their own blunders and crimes.

The biggest lie of all was that they were fine, which was always said flatly. But fine never meant fine in our family. Even when I started to gain a consciousness, a discerning mind, the women of my family's lies of omission and lies for protection, and their actions, the photographs they tucked carefully into envelopes and placed in the back of drawers, all of it enchanted and deluded me. I had fragments, half stories, sentences with verbs but no subjects. These women talked, often and loudly and over each other, but they also knew when and how to keep quiet. Their volume and rhythm depended on the topic. My grandmother and her sister and sister-in-law would go toe to toe over who made the best brisket, but people would swallow information for five decades about how they felt about men in the family.

I remember being a child and watching my mother, my first introduction into the feminine. She wore coral lipstick, a gold watch, clip-on earrings, and wedge pumps. She shaved her legs and ironed the curl right out of her hair. She smiled when she didn't feel like smiling. She was fine. She cried when she couldn't keep in the sad any longer. She wept in her shower stall in her pale pink bathroom at night when she thought I couldn't hear.

"I want to go home," she cried while the shower mist blasted her, and I lay in bed awake, pondering what this might have meant. I shivered under my blankets. No, this wasn't a home, was it, not under the absolute rule of my father. Her cries uttered what I already knew in my heart. This was a house – mortar, bricks, shackled rooftop, but this was not a home. Our house was a 1969 ranch style L-shaped suburban three bedroom sitting atop too large of a lawn for a family of four with grass allergies. No one ever wanted to mow or pick up sticks or gather leaves, but we forced ourselves to do so as to not stand out. No one in our house ever wanted to draw questions from neighbors or friends. Ours was a gulping yawn of a neighborhood that cropped up after floods of white people left the city of St. Louis for larger lawns and whiter public schools. I lived there for 12 years. But most of the time, on weekends, my mother left our house with my brother and me and drove back closer to the city center to my grandparents' home.

Their 1947 brick house was smaller and more compact, a two bedroom and an airy porch. For most of her youth, my mother slept in the dining room on a mattress, and after that she shared a room for 12 years with her grandmother. Most Jewish families referred to grandmothers as "bubbe," but my mother mispronounced that name as a child. So, my great-grandmother Esther became Bobby, and Esther, a heroic queen's name, was forgotten. Bobby was blind, but she could still quickly defeather a chicken. All the women worked in kitchens, their own or in restaurants, but their hands never betrayed this. Their fingers were nimble and their hands soft and velvety. They knew their way around coffee pots, skillets, knives and graters, potatoes, and dough. They worked quickly in kitchens that had the perpetual smell of sautéed onion, a smell I still today associate with love.

These days I no longer ingest their rich, salty food: spaghetti with thick, oniony, homemade sauce, kamish bread with strawberry jelly and cinnamon, matzah ball soup made with chicken fat, and always, Dr. Brown's cream sodas. My grandfather was a butcher and my grandmother a vegetarian, but they made this work. She asked him to taste her soups because she would not slurp them herself. Years of going without meat as a child transformed her to me as a champion of animal rights, though this was never true. My grandmother whistled as she cooked and baked. It drove others out of the kitchen, but I stayed. She taught me how to use a frying pan, how to knead dough, and how to make the best of things within the kitchen walls. Hers were black and white tile, and the kitchen her laboratory and fortress, an impenetrable bubble of safety for me for part of each week.

Like my mother, I also longed to escape our house where the rules and regulations and punitive consequences always hung over us. One could never escape our father's rigid and mathematical requirements: towels had to be folded in perfect right angles; canned goods alphabetized; shoes neatly lined up in closets. Children didn't take naturally to these directives, but threats of violence and actual violence would make them obey. We could not drop ice cubes or spill milk. Wallpaper could not be touched with small dirty fingers. We fished the remote control out of the couch every day at 5 p.m. before he stepped through the door after his workday as an accountant, tallying numbers and preparing perfected records. Everything had its place in our house, and he could walk through the rooms in his dark suit and know within seconds what was out of tune. We always waited with breaths held, going over our actions of the last hours. Did we forget to throw away a banana peel? Did someone leave an opened can of Diet Coke in the fridge? What would he find? Our thoughts were those of the deeply guilty.

He probably hadn't always been this way. When he was young and worked in grocery stores and aced tests and charmed my mother with a joke at a house party. He was a mystery, a puzzle to (never) be solved by her. He was perhaps a clever man to date. But the financial and emotional demands of establishing a family didn't require cleverness, and his only way to manage us all became an endless demand of orders.

Before meeting my father, a dentist was interested in my mother. Perhaps he wore thick glasses. Perhaps he carried a handkerchief even though it was 1972. My mom was not interested. I know a lot of nice dentists. My cousin is one of them. I wonder what life would have been like had my mom had a cold and needed a handkerchief. But no. She went to a party, and my father made a joke. My father had two sisters and two half-sisters and a mother he never, ever spoke of or talked with; this should have been a flag. In Jewish families, you had siblings and parents you couldn't stand, but you still talked to them 15 times a day. But my father never valued words much; they had no currency.

Day to day with my father was a stark contrast to time spent with my grandparents. One could eat an ice cream cone on the couch at our grandparents' home. One could leave shoes in the doorway and sweaters on chairs. They never had toys around, so my brother and I busied ourselves drawing pictures with black and blue pens on notebooks meant for grocery lists. As we drew, we were doted upon and talked to with dignity. Did the Shayna Punem (pretty face, as my grandmother called me despite my small squinting eyes and gummy smile) want vanilla or chocolate? Drinks with crushed ice or without? Lace or wool? So many questions and options and my choices mattered to this woman, my grandmother, who noted all of our preferences with care in a Rolodex in her mind. She recalled them at her weekly grocery shopping visits and garage sale runs.

I look back on this house now, this home, with love and loss, knowing how the story ends. Time passed. Bobby died, my grandparents died, and they left an empty house rotting with mold. No one had funds to repair it or hold on to it, so we let it go, too. My father died after using up his allotted number of lifetime words, and there is no one left to punish me now. And I'm fine.

Everyone leaves my city—even me. It has been many years since I put eyes on the brick home on Dorset Avenue with the wobbly gate. Neighborhoods emptied out, white flight again and again and again. The donut effect, urban historians said. Euphemism. Lawns turned to weed, 40 closed schools still stand, broken glass in their hallways, black mold on their walls. My brother and I fled a handful of times, seeking distance to put between us and the uncanny quiet of our childhoods.

But our mother is still there. She will never leave. She drinks her morning coffee, returns library books, and goes to various public meetings, taking notes. I picture her, her coral lipstick, a low hat, taking notes in her secretary shorthand as she did back in the '70s, notes only she can decipher. She kisses her photographs and tucks herself in at night. She does not sleep at night. She remembers.

Mind of Summer/Garden Gnome (after Wallace Stevens)

by Sharon Hilberer

Sharon Hilberer grew up in Pittsburgh, PA and attended school in Ohio before landing in Minnesota to work in the Minneapolis Public Schools. A language geek from the get-go, her poems spring from overheard and remembered conversations and are rooted in the life of the neighborhood. Sharon's writing is found mostly in her friends' in-boxes, but also occasionally in publications including Kosmos Quarterly, Wising Up Press, *and the* Martin Lake Journal.

Today in the mid-afternoon pause
under the slow sun in a sky pale with heat
I believe I have arrived at the mind of summer

for I have been warm for a long time,
pressed on by thick air seething with cicadas
my joints well-oiled and loose, a languid lying-back

while the grass heads ripen and bend down,
fat squash loll and swell under leafy cover,
wild blue morning glories running rampant over all

as goldenrod spills onto the path,
sunflowers nod high up in a cloud of bees,
finches dip and twist, busy at the silky thistles

and small tireless spiders work their webs
this watcher simply sits watching everything,
the everything that is here in the fullness of the end of August.

Three Poems

by John Dorsey

John Dorsey lived for several years in Toledo, Ohio. He is the author of several collections of poetry, including Teaching the Dead to Sing: The Outlaw's Prayer *(Rose of Sharon Press, 2006),* Sodomy is a City in New Jersey *(American Mettle Books, 2010),* Tombstone Factory *(Epic Rites Press, 2013),* Appalachian Frankenstein *(GTK Press, 2015)* Being the Fire *(Tangerine Press, 2016),* Shoot the Messenger *(Red Flag Poetry, 2017),* Your Daughter's Country *(Blue Horse Press, 2019),* Which Way to the River: Selected Poems 2016-2020 *(OAC Books, 2020),* Afterlife Karaoke *(Crisis Chronicles Press, 2021), and* Sundown at the Redneck Carnival *(Spartan Press, 2022). His work has been nominated for the Pushcart Prize, Best of the Net, and the Stanley Hanks Memorial Poetry Prize. He was the winner of the 2019 Terri Award given out at the Poetry Rendezvous. He may be reached at archerevans@yahoo.com.*

The Ghosts of Washington Square Mall

every morning the janitor
wipes dust off the lips
of a dead soap opera star

a young girl places flowers in fresh dirt
in memory of 1987
her god is a time machine

big hair
big hearts

mall walkers who waited tables here
before dropping out of college
to hide behind the fences
of suburban wastelands

the wall outside the bar
is the only thing that's left

a carousel that doesn't move
to the music
of the past.

Pistol City Elergy
for merritt walden

you can forget about the blues
the street corners that sing
about the days
that have already lived & died
inside your heart
before you ever got to know them
words that got choked out
watching a flower grow mad in the heat
while austin indiana walks around
with its hands in its pockets
fists clenched
like the ghost of a wild bird
waiting for you
to say something beautiful.

Reading Allen Ginsberg in Eat N Park in 1992
for george rouse

the best minds of my generation
craved gravy fries
in trailers with empty ice boxes

riding bicycles
into the heart
of loneliness

with fathers who had metal plates
in their heads

fathers with flashbacks

fathers who never knew
what they wanted to do

or exactly what it was
they were running from
in the supermarket parking lot
on sundays

at war with poverty & silence
still raging

their sons becoming
punching bags
becoming scarecrows
protecting them
from their own uncertainty

their baby faces
smiling back
in the reflection
of a dirty
coffee cup.

Laments of a Time Witch
by Jasmine Shea Townsend

Jasmine was born in 1992 and has lived in Northwest Ohio her entire life. After receiving her BA in English (with a focus in creative writing), she spent a month studying abroad in Japan before returning to Toledo to start graduate school. She fell in love with ballroom dance (a passion she shares with the narrator of this piece). For the next two years, she balanced dance and my studies. She competed in collegiate ballroom dance competitions across the Midwest, collecting ribbons with her partner, and in 2015, she graduated from UT with an MA in English literature. She is an adjunct professor at Lourdes, teaching mainly Introduction to Literature and Professional Writing.

When I wake up from my nap, I exist outside of time. I sit up, and the world around me moves like I'm underwater. To tell you the truth, I want to go back to sleep for the rest of the day and into the night and finish out the month in a cocoon of blankets.

That's a lie. It wouldn't be blissful at all because every time I close my eyes, I see my sister's face. But maybe it would be better than the ache of missing her in my waking life. My throat feels stiff, and I can't remember the last time I spoke. I haven't danced in days.

I shoulder on my jacket, step into my rainboots, and march across the plashy field into the woods. Raindrops filter through the canopy of leaves, feeling cool on my face and hands.

Past the graves of beloved pets, past the tree into which Tristian and I scratched our initials all those years ago, there is Amy's sad, little tombstone sinking into the mud. Amy, the twin sister who was meant to have half my power and got none of it. Amy, who worked hard and never blamed me for keeping all her potential for myself in the womb. Amy, whose last words to me were, "Help me find Lucas, will you?"

Our cat escaped and clamored high into a tree he was too afraid to descend. Amy shouted, "There you are!" as she climbed up the branches. I didn't see it happen, but I heard the branch crack and the twigs snapping as she screamed. The silence that followed that horrible, dull thump bit through me like frost. Inconsolable dread sank into my bones like melting ice even before I started running to her.

I miss her.

The tombstone is lopsided, and I stoop to fix it myself, but it's too heavy. Our little brother, too young to understand anything, begged me through tears to go back and stop her, to bring her back. I told him my powers don't work that way, that the past is permanent. That death is permanent.

I am the most powerful time witch alive, and I am completely powerless.

Amy, lacking abilities, was a kitchen witch. Our mother is a bio witch with a specialization in botany, so they worked closely. I liked watching them laugh together in the garden after coming home from my weekend private lessons. Suddenly, I'm thinking of Amy's smiling face peeking from behind potted pink and white azaleas. Our mother works her magic to sustain our garden—aromatic basil and mint, fragrant hyacinths and gardenias, plump tomatoes and peaches. She would also extract the best, purest oils so Amy could make the best, purist potions, elixirs, serums, and creams. I could have had any tea in existence, but my favorite of Amy's was her lavender chamomile right before snuggling into bed with Lucas curled up at my side, warm and purring. I think about him now, sulking under my bed as he's made a habit of doing more often since Amy's death, as if he could sense it were his fault.

Footsteps squish in the soggy forest floor, and I pause everything—a bird mid-song, raindrops suspended mid-fall—to investigate my surroundings. It's sweet-faced Tristan frozen in his approach, and when I unpause, he continues making his way toward me.

"I went to check up on you," he says. "You weren't at home, so I figured you might be here."

Droplets trickle from the rim of his hood, and I'm hyper aware of my braids and clothes, all soaked through.

"You're going to catch cold," he says.

And what if I do? I want to say. It would give me an excuse to stay in bed. I'm tempted to pause again and leave, but he doesn't deserve that. He didn't deserve it the first time I did it.

Back then, Tristan led me down a path between rows of cherry blossom trees in bloom to a white gazebo bordered by rose bushes. Our instructor had worked us hard that morning on a difficult routine designed to dazzle the judges from our little spot on the competition floor. It was Tristan's idea to cool down with a stroll through the botanical gardens. When we reached the gazebo, the old wood groaned under our feet, and I admired the cherry blossom petals playing in the spring breeze, a contrast to the gray sky threatening rain.

"It's nice," I said. I planned to tell Amy about it later.

"Right? I love this view," Tristan said.

I turned to him. "And that's what you brought me here for? The view?"

Tristan has kind, drooping eyes, like a puppy. He averted his gaze, considering his next words carefully. My heartbeat sped, not in anticipation, but in fear. I knew he had tried to make the idea for a stroll seem spontaneous, but the nerves tugging at the ends of his words when he suggested it indicated that he'd been planning it for a while. He has always been a terrible actor off the dance floor.

"I was just thinking about our tree," he said.

"It's a nice tree," I said, stupidly.

He looked at me with such sincerity in his dark brown eyes. Such earnestness. My urge to run began with the first break of drizzle.

Tristan continued. "I know that was years ago, but that feeling never went away."

We'd both been eleven years old when we'd scratched out initials into that tree, six years before the birth of my little brother, fourteen years before the death of my sister. Since then, I had watched him date girls for whom his feelings ran lukewarm at best, though he didn't usually realize it, and a small part of me always knew why.

"Tristan, I can't."

"You don't even know what I'm going to say."

I regarded him—his soft curls, his cherubic mouth. "I think I do, though."

I had never felt anything for anyone, not in the way Tristan felt for me, and it wasn't for lack of trying.

A light rain tapped on the roof of the gazebo. I paused time and replayed our walk up the path through the cherry blossoms. Our apparitions from where I stood in the gazebo seem content enough— my smile placid, his tinged with a nervousness I pretended not to notice.

When our apparitions caught up to us, I walked away and didn't unpause until I got home. Amy, sensing my distress, brewed us a pot of tea.

I'm honestly surprised that that hadn't ruined our friendship. It was a wholly inconsiderate thing to do, and when I cried from the weight of my cowardice and guilt, Amy hugged me until I dozed on her shoulder.

"I'm sorry," I say now.

Tristan looks confused. "For what?"

"For what I did a month ago," I say. "At the gazebo."

He reaches out and places a hand on my shoulder. "Don't worry about that right now."

"But I never apologized, and it's long overdue, and I don't even deserve for you to be here for me right now."

I resent my lip for trembling as I say this. I have a feeling that if I cry now, I won't be able to stop.

I could leap forward a hundred years from now. The thought is fleeting, but I could grieve alone in a time where there would be no one left alive to disappoint. Amy's grave would be covered by earth, moss, and ivy, and no one would ever know anyone lay there, except for me. But why punish my loved ones with another death?

Tristan places his free hand on my other shoulder. "I shouldn't have sprung that up on you the way I did."

"And I shouldn't have abandoned you like some shitty friend." The tears bubble over. "I'm so sorry, Tristan, I really am. It's just that I can't give you what you want, and I was so scared I wouldn't be able to make things right and that—"

Tristan pulls me into a hug, which I graciously accept.

"—and that we wouldn't be friends anymore."

"Shh," he said. "Breathe."

"I love you."

"I love you, too. Let's get you out of the rain."

The routine we were practicing the day of the gazebo incident would have won us ribbons. Our instructor had choreographed for us a brooding waltz that demanded so much of us. Linger a little longer here on this note. Hold the pose there a little longer. Tristan's strong frame swept me in grand twirls, one after the other. He spun me under his arm, his posture erect and impeccable, and we leaned in, faces close enough to kiss, with soft, doe-eyed gazes and smiles warm enough to brighten the whole room—we really had to sell it to the judges—and clasped our hands together. Then we detonated, fanning out our arms and turning with flourish to face the studio mirror. Tristan squeezed my hand. Our instructor applauded. I was tired and sore, but I was deeply pleased with us. Afterward, I was dabbing sweat from around my neck when Tristan wanted to know how I'd feel about a walk.

***

Tristan knows where we keep all the blankets and towels. After I change into my dry clothes, he helps me dry my braids, sits me on the couch, and layers me with blankets. Apparently, I was shivering.

102

"I'll be right back," he says, and soon, I hear the kitchen cabinets opening and closing,

water boiling, vegetables minced on the chopping block. It smells like vegetable lentil soup made with ingredients from the garden.

Part of me considers joining him. The living room is a palimpsest of memories, which is why I've been avoiding it lately. I don't know if replaying my favorite moments with Amy is helping or hurting the healing process, but the temptation is stronger than my will. I scroll through the ghosts of our past selves. They're initially vivid, then fade, leaving behind afterimages of happier times. It was here that we sat on our knees, tiny brows knitted in concentration, as we painted wooden dolls in vibrant reds, greens, whites, and yellows. Much later, Amy and I fawned over our brother when he was a baby, rocking his cradle and singing gentle hymns.

Often, she would help me with my deep stretches on the floor, and in the beginning, it was fun. It stopped being fun when I noticed a hidden sourness she'd developed whenever I talked about dance. I always thought it must have been my competitive nature bordering on obsession that bothered her. If Tristan and I didn't receive the marks I thought we deserved, I'd return to the venue and replay every movement, every subtle nod of a judge's stoic head. In almost a trance, I would explain to her in detail how the couple who was chosen instead of us was actually a little off beat, or how one judge had his head bowed during a crucial moment in my and Tristan's routine. That must have grated on her. I realize how maddening I must have been, feverish as I became when I recounted these things. Now that version of myself seems a mile away. I search for more memories.

A little further forward, I mistime a memory and land on something else entirely. When this happens, it's usually our parents reading or our brother painting dolls of his own—the dull things that happen when I'm not around. But why is Tristan here? This memory must have been sometime last year because Amy's locks are pink. They are alone in the living room, sitting on the couch. I decide to let this one play.

Tristan traces his thumb across Amy's soft cheek, and she leans forward to kiss him. He pulls her closer, and she buries her slender fingers into his curls. Neither of them has told me anything about this. Where was I? They stand, and I follow their apparitions up the stairs. It's jarring seeing my sister and my best friend like this. They had both had relationships before, so I knew they'd done this sort of thing, but seeing it happen *with each other* is something too surreal to process.

They continue kissing in her room on her bed and don't bother to close the door all the way because no one else is home. When Tristan's hands begin to wander, I look away. I'm about to pause when I hear him speak.

"I'm sorry, Amy."

I look into the room, and Amy looks disappointed but understanding.

"So, you love her after all," she says.

"You okay?" Tristan says, his voice behind me.

I spin around, startled. I didn't hear him coming up the stairs. When I return my gaze to Amy's bedroom, the ghosts are gone. I turn back to Tristan. I'm hurt that neither of them mentioned this to me, that they shared this secret, but it's hard for me to feel utterly betrayed. This town is small. Who could blame either of them for trying? And now I understand Amy's reactions to my post-competition ravings. Dutiful sister that she was, she always came to see us, along with the rest of our family, and I, oblivious, had attributed her pinched expression and stiff applause to fatigue after sitting so long, watching wave after wave of flashy couples crowd the dance floor for hours. Tristan is a master at navigating, and he is a fiercely protective partner. In his arms, in his strong frame, I went wherever he twirled me. He stepped into me and I made room. If he ever stopped to hold me close, I froze obediently, sensing another couple gliding behind me. Dance is an intimate sport, and our chemistry was flawless, amorous, a convincing act perfected in part by my drive for ribbons. But Amy knew that for Tristan, it wasn't all an act. I look at him now, a million words swimming in my mouth.

"Um, soup's ready. You're out of bread, though," he says.

I can't stop myself from blurting the words. "So, you and Amy."

Tristan's chin drops until his lips part. A quiet panic buzzes around the outsides of his eyes, behind which I see the cogs whirr to life.

"Why didn't you tell me?" I say. "Why didn't either of you tell me?"

"Because I know you, and we knew it would bother you, but you'd never say anything."

I don't want to admit that he's probably right. I don't want to admit that had I known, my performance wouldn't have been the same, knowing Amy was shooting daggers from her seat in the stands. But this wouldn't have been the first time either of them would have had to force me to talk. One or both of them would have pestered me, and I would have begrudgingly opened up, and we could have figured something out!

"I'm not bothered that it happened," I say. "I'm bothered that you kept it from me!"

Maybe I'm misreading his expression, but I detect disappointment.

He regards me with a steadfast gaze. "So, it doesn't bother you at all, Amy and me. Which, for the record, never took off."

I throw my hands up. "Well, if you both would have been happy, I would have been happy for you both. But you were holding onto hope for something that will never happen."

When I told Tristan that it wasn't that I didn't love anyone, it was that I *couldn't,* he didn't suggest in a sly way that I was somehow broken or simply mistaken or, my favorite, a "late bloomer," like an orchid that grew tall and green but hadn't yet matured enough to produce its concupiscent petals.

I hadn't even told Amy yet. Truth be told, I didn't know I'd be telling him that night. Tristan and I were sixteen and seventeen years old, and he was walking me home from the spring formal, where he'd accompanied me as a friend-date. The moon cast its frosty glow on the ancient wrought-iron fence encircling the courtyard. Elsewhere throughout the little campus, groups of friends hung out under trees or laughed and joked on the benches or in the grass. Couples kissed discreetly and meekly, probably afraid (and a little thrilled by the possibility) a chaperone would round the corner and spot them. Inside, the band was packing up, and chaperones were trying to shoo teenagers home so they could go home, too.

Tristan took my confession in stride. He wrapped an arm around my shoulder and squeezed. I suspect all hope he had for us becoming an *us* had died just then, all but one resilient glimmer. I look at him now, in my house, as the soup gets cold, and see only a faint line of smoke where the glimmer used to be.

Suddenly, he says, "Can I admit something to you?"

"What kind of a question is that?" I say. "Always."

"You're right. A part of me always hoped. I'm ashamed of that, but it's true." He shifts a little on his feet. "I fell in love with your laugh first. And then your intellect. And it's really the dancing that made it hard—so much so that I thought about quitting, but I knew it would devastate you. Your following is effortless, your lines are gorgeous, and when you look at me like, I don't know, like you're in love with me—"

"It's the story of the dance, Tristan."

"I know, let me finish. When you look at me like that, you're so good at it that sometimes I believe it." He closes his eyes, opens them again. "Amy and I couldn't have been happy because she had your beauty, but not your grace and your laugh and all that other stuff. You mind. It was always you." He sighs. "I didn't tell you because I was heartbroken and ashamed of thinking she could replace you, and that's the truth."

I can't think of anything to say, so I take his hands in mine. I don't know what else to do.

"You told me a piece of yourself, and I was just like everyone else—pretending it wasn't real to suit my own selfish narrative, and I'm sorry."

I shook my head. "No, you weren't like everyone else. I think you really wanted to believe me. We can't help how we feel."

"Now I'm the one afraid of our friendship crumbling," he says.

I crack a smile. "Are you kidding? It can only get stronger from here."

I don't know how long we embraced. Hours, years, centuries?

***

My paternal grandmother is also a bio witch, but with a specialization in animal communication. She said that before Amy and I were born, the time ability hadn't resurfaced in the family in over two hundred years, and here her son's wife was going to bring two into the world.

I curl up in bed without having dinner. My parents move around downstairs, but no one is talking. Lucas emerges from underneath my bed with a long stretch and saunters to his food bowl, the tip of his tail curled in uncertainty. He sniffs at the kibble he likely hasn't touched all day before he finally deigns to eat. After we picked him up at the shelter and my grandmother came by to meet him, she said, "This isn't the family cat. This is the girls' cat."

"Lucas," I say when he's done eating. "Come here, sweet boy."

His tail perks up and he hops into bed with me, purring. He is a white-and-orange cat, so he's easy to see in the dark, and I watch him paw around on the bed until he finds my stomach, which he kneads.

I pet him. "Do you miss her? I miss her so much."

Lucas lies on my torso and licks my chin.

The last time the three of us siblings where all together at our grandmother's, we were helping her tend to her many birds—lime green parrotlets, budgerigars of every color, blushing cockatiels.

Then, our little brother decided to ask, "What happens when you stop time?"

"I don't stop time," I said. "I pause it."

"Oh." He was quite for a while. Then, "So what happens when you pause it?"

"Everything and everyone pauses but me. And when time resumes—I mean, when everything starts moving again—you won't even notice I've paused you."

But later that day, my grandmother asked me, "There are moments you wished you could stop, aren't there?"

It's physically impossible, but any time witch who's suffered moments of unfathomable darkness has undoubtedly thought about it at least once. What happens when you disappear without actually going anywhere and you take the whole world with you, and no one will ever know anything ever again? As the time witch who would have caused this hypothetical cessation of existence, I would likely be aware of each countless second of eternity ticking by but would be unable to do anything about it, like the most nightmarish sleep paralysis.

"Who hasn't?" I said.

"Well, sooner or later, time stops for all of us," she said. "No point in rushing to get there. But you pause when you need to, you hear me? Pause for as long as you need. But no matter how bad things get, you can't stop."

I close my eyes and run a hand down Lucas's back as he continues to purr. He feels almost like a warm weighted blanket. He rests his head on my chest and purrs until he falls asleep. I decide first thing in the morning to pick calendulas, violas, and pansies for Amy. Then, I'm going to visit the studio.

The Show
by Devon Ortega

Devon Ortega is an artist and writer living in Pickerington, Ohio with her husband and four children. She obtained a bachelor's degree from The Ohio State University and a master's degree in creative writing at Ohio University. She was the recipient of the 2011 Gertrude Lucille Robinson Award for her poetry series Tavern at Ten. *Her poetry and short fiction have appeared in* Barren Magazine, Azure Magazine, *and several anthologies. She currently serves as the fantasy editor at* The Worlds Within *magazine.*

Colin hadn't needed anyone in his whole life, and he certainly didn't need the loaf of a woman who sat on his back porch screaming obscenities at him. He took another swing at the telephone pole with the axe and the resulting reverberations up his arms were satisfying as much as they energized him to swing again and again.

Penny (she went by Penny, now), sat in a rusted out plastic lawn chair older than she was, half of the pink tubes on the seat had snapped ages ago but still hung uselessly at its sides. She kicked off her house shoes and propped her feet up on the warped porch railing. "Hope you give yourself a hernia doing that, you stupid shit. Hope the damn pole falls straight on your big fuckin' head."

Colin was tired of paying the bills, paying his dues at work and still having to pay attention to his damn kid and bitch wife when he got home. Terry, his boy, threw a bagel bite at his own father's head when he told the little punk to go pick up all the dog shit in the yard. They didn't even have a dog but somehow there was always an alarming amount of dog shit in their yard—a variety of sizes from a variety of dogs. Colin could never figure out where it all came from, and it pissed him off.

Terry was watching TV. Rotting what little pea brain he had away instead of listening to his father, stuffing those pizza things into his face so fast the real surprise was he wasted one to use as a projectile on his father. When it slid from Colin's chin, he watched it go down his shirt, leaving a trail of red and spatting on the floor. And Colin, in typical Colin fashion, lost his cool. He tried to tip over the TV, but he knocked one of Penny's Precious Moments off the top of the console and that finally made her lazy ass pay attention. One second she's smoking over the sink, looking at the Hollywood

Gossip! magazine she always seemed to have an endless supply of money for, the next second she was screaming about how those statues were "heirlooms" from her mama and for every statue he broke, she would go over to his mama's house and break one of her heirloom frog princess statues. Joke was on her though because unless she broke his mama's glucose monitor, he couldn't care less about what she smashed.

Colin tried to maintain focus- the boy had thrown a bagel bite at him. Colin could feel the grease from those tiny pepperonis still oily on his chin, where it struck. He also watched too much television. Colin hated that Godforsaken thing, television. Watching his wife and son mindlessly shovel cheese poofs into their mouths at night, the flickering eerie light keeping them both stupidly transfixed. Penny had inherited the damn thing after her grandmama passed away. The old crone left Penny the broke down blue Lincoln Continental in the drive and her mammoth, bulge-bellied console TV. Both capital H Heirlooms.

Penny could never part with anything, even if it went against everything Colin stood for. He never had a TV growing up and he was just fine. But everything was an heirloom to Penny. It was probably for the best Colin didn't tip it over. He imagined it would spark and shatter, maybe start fire and, while the thought of a dramatic, mini-explosion sounded just fine to him, Penny would have a shit fit. Probably throw him out again. Penny might be as mean as a fixed cat with a Q-tip in its ass, but she was the love of his life. And if Colin couldn't break the TV, which was apparently made of industrial grade paneling and protected by a hundred teardrop-eyed, porcelain albino children, he would fix his son another way. Long story short, that's how Colin came to be out in his back yard trying to knock down the power lines.

***

Penny watched her common-law asshole strike the power pole over and over with a level of energy he had rarely used in bed. It had been five minutes of pure exertion and he hadn't passed out snoring yet, so she knew he was either drunk or had true passion for something for once.

She lit the last cigarette in her pack of Kiss Cherry Super Slims and watched the flesh on Colin's back jiggle underneath his sweat soaked shirt with each slam with the axe. She inhaled the cloying yet bitter flavor, knowing it was her job to stop the moronic ox from chopping down the world but in the way that a mother enjoys the peace of a child up to no good, the silence before it all goes to shit,

Penny inhaled and watched as Colin tried to best a hunk of wood 35 feet his superior.

Penny's mind drifted, looking at the dry grass and staring at the almost setting sun hoping maybe if she blinded herself, she could get a prescription for some Oxy. Donna had given her some after her gallbladder surgery and Penny sure liked those. Yeah, the only thing to make this evening better would be some Oxy. Maybe a little pot in a pinch. As it was, all she had was half a Kiss Cherry. She'd have to send Terry down to the market to get her some more.

"Terry! Bring mama her big purse!" Penny flicked the remainder of the cigarette into the yard and waited, noticing that Colin was no longer continuing his assault on the telephone pole but instead was marching across the yard to the neighbor's house. Their neighbor, Possum (no one ever told her his God-given name), standing on the crumbling concrete patio behind his own house, wiping his forehead with what looked to Penny to be a pair of men's underwear. She needed another smoke for this interaction between the men. It never went well when those two hot-headed morons went up against each other. "Goddammit, Terry! My big purse!" She struggled out of the ratty lawn chair, the ergonomics of it good for keeping her ass available to the breeze but not efficient for getting out of.

Penny hurried into the house, the screen door slamming into the siding. She kept forgetting the spring was broken. The big purse sat slovenly on the kitchen table, lazy brown folds flopping over like a deflated pleather balloon. Similarly, her son sat seemingly melted into the couch, more invested in whatever flickered on the screen than he ever would be to schoolwork or obedience or even hygiene.

Penny dug into the cavernous bag hoping for a carcinogenic miracle and found a single halfie left in a crushed soft pack from a week ago. "Amen," she said. She wadded up a five-dollar bill and used it as a projectile to peg Terry in the head. Varsity softball all four years of high school and she never missed. She half joked it was the only thing she learned in school, but she knew in her heart it was probably more truth than joke.

Terry blinked twice and looked at his mother. "Cigarettes?" he said. His lips were orange from cheese puffs.

"Yeah. You eat all the poofs? Get more poofs." She handed him a few more dollars in change from the bottom of her bag. "And hustle!" Penny yelled the last part before Terry could protest he wanted to finish whatever he was watching. Terry might not listen to his daddy but when mama needed her smokes, he knew being expeditious was the only option.

"Mama, you missed it. Some kid just got shot on People's Court! There was blood and everything!" Terry talked as he stuffed the money into the front pocket of his jean shorts.

"No, baby, people don't get shot on The People's Court. You was probably watching Divorce Court. Or Superior Court or something. Now, get on. Go get my shit, honey." Penny struggled to light the halfie without burning the tip of her nose off. She inhaled and went back out to finish watching her own show.

***

The sweat raining down Colin's back was making his pants slip down so he struggled to adjust them while still sticking his chest out like a prize-fighting cock. "Gimmie your goddam chainsaw then so I can saw it up proper and you can have your fucking nap!"

Possom, equally pot-bellied and sweaty, swayed back and forth in a way that indicated either some level of intoxication or an uncomfortable case of swamp ass. "Like hell, you piece of shit. You'd just sell it off for marijuana and I'd never see it again." Possom articulated the word like Mary-watta. He wiped the sweat from his ripening, bald head with what were likely a dirty pair of his own tighty whities. Yellowies.

"Well maybe I'll just chop the damn pole down with your wife's hatchet face then!" Colin moved like he was going to navigate past Possum to fetch Missus Possum who, despite her heavy frame had a face narrow and pointy enough to split lumber.

As Colin approached, Possum flung out his arms in a strangely graceful display of self-defense. In this process of quick motion of seemingly ineffective aggression, he either intentionally or unintentionally punched Colin in a sort of back-handed uppercut with the fist holding the balled-up underwear inside.

Colin, momentarily blinded by having his nose shoved upwards into his eye socket blinked back tears as blood began pouring out of his nose. He blinked again and swiped away the hot mess dripping from his face. By the time he gained his bearings, the screen door was slamming behind Possum as he scurried back into his house and locked the door. Possum peered sheepishly out of the window for a moment before dropping the fabric from his hand and, Colin assumed, running to hide behind his human shield of a wife.

Instead of sense being knocked into Colin, somehow more rage was rattled loose, and he screamed pathetically as he searched the long, half dead grass for the axe he dropped when getting punched by someone's underwear.

111

He continued screaming after he found the axe. After he picked it up. And after he ran full speed up to Possum's house and began to hack at whatever area he came upon. First, Colin chopped at the side of the house, the siding clanging and bouncing the axe dangerously as it recoiled from the metal. He was still screaming when he chopped the screen door off its hinges and flung it into the yard in a satisfying display of out-of-control masculinity.

He continued loudly screaming and chopping, the sweat making it difficult to hold on to the axe handle, but he didn't stop. Not even when he got wise and axed out all the windows in the back of the house. Not when he shattered the glass in the front either. Not even when the police car pulled up, the officer staring in disbelief as a deranged, sunburned man went mano a mano with a house that was showing no signs of fighting back.

***

Penny had migrated herself and her lawn chair to the gravel drive to watch the insane man she lived with chop at her neighbor's house. She was on her second beer by the time the cop car showed up. Terry waved jubilantly from the back seat, cheese poof dust covering his fingers and lips.

Sonofabitch. Penny downed the rest of her Coors and slung the can into the yard behind her. She struggled out of the busted chair and began saying, "No, Colin! Stop!" Half-heartedly though, as if to only prevent from implicating herself in some way. The show was getting a little out of hand. Less People's Court. More Superior Court.

Colin finally noticed that there was a world spinning around him, things going on outside of his maddened, relentless attack on a house and stopped chopping. He looked over at Penny, her penciled on brows up so high they were almost touching her hairline, eyes wide- looking at him. He noticed the red and blue lights illuminating the neighborhood and out of the corner of his eye, saw the blue uniform cautiously approaching.

Without thinking, Colin dropped the axe and turned to face the officer. The cop opened his mouth but before he could say a word, Colin turned and, with some reserve of energy he had never had before in his life, he ran.

"Stop," the officer said, immediately giving chase.

Penny sighed and looked away. Terry was still in the back of the squad car pressing his face against the window and licking it, cheese dust fingerprints all over the once clean glass. When he saw her looking at him, he said, "Hi, mama! I got you your Kisses!" He then stood up and pressed his ass cheeks to the window shouting, "Full moon!"

Penny walked to the cop car and opened the door. Terry plopped out, ass first onto the pavement. "Gimmie them smokes and get your ass into the house. Your daddy's gonna need your seat here in a minute."

Terry pulled up his pants and ran inside without another word. She figured it was about time for Quantum Leap to come on and while she didn't think Terry truly understood the show, he thought it was funny when Sam Beckett was forced to be a woman for an episode. *Yeah, actually try it for a minute and see how funny it is*, she always thought.

By the time the screen door slapped behind Terry, the officer reappeared, guiding the handcuffed Colin towards his squad car. He didn't get far. Penny knew he wouldn't.

"It hurts to put my arms down," was all Colin said to her as he passed, the smell of rank sweat and grass and defeat said far more than he ever could anyhow.

"I'm not paying bail!" Penny said.

"Fine. Don't." Colin shouted back, not even attempting to look over his shoulder at her.

"You're going to rot in there if I don't!"

"I said I don't give a shit!" Colin stumbled and the officer kept him from falling—the fatigue of trying to chop down the world finally catching up to him.

"I ain't going to wait for you!" Penny's hands shook as she fiddled a Kiss Super Slim out of the package.

Colin didn't say anything else before the door of the squad car closed him inside. The officer sat in the drivers seat, speaking into his walkie. Penny stared at Colin, willing him to look up at her, to give her one last look before he was gone back to the place where everybody knew his name. *If jail was a bar, Colin would be Norm Peterson*, Penny thought. After what felt like an eternity, Colin finally looked up. He turned his head to look at Penny one last time.

Penny sneered at him and flipped him the bird. With nothing left to say, she turned and stomped towards the house, slamming the door behind her. Her cigarette went out during the staring contest, so she paused to relight it, leaning back against the cool, textured wall of her hallway.

"Mama, I sure liked riding in that cop car. He drove me home and I didn't even have to tell him where I lived. He just knew!" Terry hopped a little when he said this; the boy—a bit big for eleven—

rarely showed that level of excitement and rattled the plates on the wall when he jumped.

"Of course he did, Terry-tot." Penny rubbed her temples, wanting the child to not be right there, talking, but she needed to ask. "You tell that man daddy was hacking at the phone pole?"

"Uh huh. And he put his hand on me and called me son. It was weird as hell." Terry was trying out some new words and "hell" was the most recent boundary testing one.

"Go watch your show," Penny said, rubbing at her temples while she decided whether or not it was worth it to cry.

"You coming? Dr. Beckett's a pregnant lady this week. You gotta come see, he looks dumb as hell." Terry turned and ran back to the living room, his heavy footfalls rattling the whole house.

"Don't say hell," Penny said softly, mostly to herself.

She didn't know when the cop was going to come pounding on the door. She didn't know what she would even say this time. Penny didn't want to think about it anymore. She didn't want to think about anything. What she wanted was to see Scott Bakula in a dress. *Try it for a minute.*

"I'm really going to miss that asshole," she said, more or less meaning it. Penny wiped her eyes then walked into the living room to wait for what was going to happen next.

Two Poems
by Amanda McGuire

Amanda McGuire's work appears in This Quarantine Life: A COVID-19 Era Comics Anthology, Hotel Amerika, NOON: journal of the short poem, Cream City Review, the Toledo Museum of Art, *and other literary spaces. She teaches and lives in Bowling Green, Ohio with her spouse and dog.*

Trying to Draw My Hand

First I place it just-so on the table On the sketchpad nothing yet I would rather be in bed Instead I hear the scratch of pencil snore of the fat dog so many crickets between the sprinkles of an impeding storm Only with years more practice will I be good at this But I see my life here "You'll sit next to your spouse while they are making something." One niece started high school is thriving in crew theatre clubs and band The other started college and is lonely in her urban apartment at a commuter campus Within my thumbnails are the thumbnails of my story When I close my eyes the lines make more sense On a sticky Florida day a palm reader stared at my high-schooler hands and nodded approval My perspective is one point I always wish for three Though the medieval fair was boring af back then that palm reading was a fun story to tell drunk Now I rely on arcs and panels to tell stories I use my own hands for making Now My spouse shuffles in with a morning nod Sits down at the table with his laptop At least part of the fortune came true

My Earrings Are A Math Equation

When my drawing teacher says It's all geometry I mute the Zoom lecture What is looming over us is despair Not a box with lines and vanishing point that moves beyond what we can see Look That bird doesn't care about me walking pounds of grass seed from the detached garage to the front yard thinking *The Jizz Fairy* from Red Hood *might be real* My teacher's tech freezes That's when I unmute That's when I hear someone whistle *Everywhere* Before I look I know It's that annoying Fleetwood Mac fan who drinks wine out of a coffee mug during class The sky whirls with disappointment In my imagination I draw Stevie Nicks lacing roller skates She's animated I've decided Yeah the Jizz Fairy is real I only know because I used to be a drunk too A bike A lightning bolt A bird All those Zoom boxes are panels in the longest graphic novel yet to be written Nothing is adding up and yet something is complete

The Dissolution of Rebekah Stern

by B.L. Makiefsky

B.L. Makiefsky was the winner of the 2012 Michigan Writers Cooperative Press chapbook contest, for the short story collection Fathers and Sons. *Among publications his work has been featured in (or is forthcoming) are the* Detroit Free Press, Dunes Review, Thoughtful Dog, Pithead Chapel, Brilliant Flash Fiction, Fiction Southeast, Flash Fiction Magazine, Hypertext Magazine, the Great Lakes Review, On The Run *and* jewishfiction.net.

The September sun was hot and the nights warm and the market good, so the pickle harvest continued. The migrant workers had finished for the day and the fields that Rebekah Stern drove past were empty except for the white plastic buckets they had left, scattered like seagulls in hills of faded green and ochre. Rebekah was anxious. Time—defined in Bear County by the harvest and measured not in weeks or days but in bins and lugs and crates—fell heavily upon her. She felt unmoored living so far north, yet unmoved by her mother's entreaties to return home, downstate. She had become what she thought she had wanted to be: a state-employed social worker in the Lake Michigan fruit belt. Above all, she had wanted to show the farmworkers that she was an advocate for human rights and the dignity of manual labor. That even though she'd been born into privilege, she understood.

And now this. The Bear County Director of Human Services, Nelson Roy, was accusing her boyfriend, migrant crew leader Carlos Dávila, of hacking into the state's benefits system to divert food stamps and cash assistance to his friends. An agency computer was allegedly found at the church in Crystal Valley, where she was headed.

Rebekah passed a truck pulling into the cannery and thought of how going to Roy's office was not unlike entering a crawlspace. Even if you emerged without spider eggs and insect wings clinging to you, you still felt dirty. He'd ask you out, or call you out, often in the same breath. A few years older than her, the 30-year-old Roy was single, and well over six feet tall. His height, long blond hair, surfer boy good looks and tailored suits stood out in rural Stillwater, the county seat.

On a wall above the director's desk hung a portrait of the president, Ronald Reagan. Tinted floor-to-ceiling windows overlooked the building grounds and, in the distance, the bay. Roy told Rebekah there were unaccounted benefits flying out the door, and he blamed Dávila, who worked for the farmer Miles VanSlyke. Never mind that office workers were certain that Roy's secretary had her hand in the pot; Rebekah wouldn't mention that. Roy refused to ask Lansing for help. "They don't promote suckers," he said, before telling her that a janitor at St. Joseph's Church found a state computer in their basement. Maybe one, or one of several, never returned to central office in exchange for new Dells that we were promised. And never got.

Roy asked Rebekah to go to the church and investigate. He would give her the remainder of the day off, and she could start her planned trip to visit family early. "Maybe you'll run into your *friend* Carlos there," he added.

***

Rebekah thought back to spring when she was hired. She had always lived in one city or another and didn't know what to expect; the population of Stillwater was less than that of a suburban mall downstate on a Saturday afternoon. Along country roads, the daffodils pushed through what remained of the snowpack, and in the fields and orchards the mudded ruts were drying up. Not long after, migrant families arrived from South Texas to harvest the county's rich asparagus crop and her agency struggled to meet the needs— housing, for those who arrived without a commitment from a farmer; food stamps; Medicaid; and the unending parade of emergency requests. Locals didn't much work the fields anymore, and the migrant families the farmers hired relied on government benefits to supplement wages dependent on the vagaries of crops, market and weather.

From asparagus to cherries to apples the office reeled like the midway at the county fair, as farmworkers—from such places as Harlingen and Wauchula, San Juan and Edinburg—tried their luck at various games, determined to turn the tables and call the chips theirs. Rebekah learned two things that summer: Clients who understood the rules beat the house; and even the most larcenous among them rarely understood the hand they'd been dealt. She was proud of herself for figuring this out; and she was ashamed, too, for her part in a system that turned honorable persons into beggars, and beggars into thieves. *What am I eligible for?* had become, in sickness and health, *what am I entitled to?*

Carlos Dávila thought they were entitled to plenty, and he and Roy had sparred all summer. Ruggedly handsome, his dark face weathered by sun, wind and road, he was the first to reach out to Rebekah. By strawberries, they'd become a couple. From him, she would learn of droughts and mites, *Cinco de Mayo* and the *coming Día de los muertos.* With him, she'd go to church weddings, baptisms, Easter egg hunts and festival dances.

But Rebekah's upper-level courses hadn't covered the misuse of state property or illegally diverted funds, she thought as she turned off the two-lane this day. From a hill above St. Joseph's Church, she watched the dust from tractors settle over the dirt road below. She had wanted to tell Roy that she indeed hoped Carlos was there. They hadn't seen each other in four days, and that felt like four days too many.

She parked her car and walked to a side door of the church. The building was made of brick and stucco, with a small cemetery on the side where dew-washed crosses glistened in the morning light. Someone unlatched the door when she knocked, and it creaked open. Rebekah shouted out a hello, but whoever had let her in had disappeared. She thought she heard a child scampering away. She followed the steep cement steps down into the cellar, her eyes slowly adjusting to the dimness. The chill made her shudder. She saw people scurrying about a long table, boxing computers and assorted hardware. Carlos emerged from the shadows.

"Who let her in?" he said, in a tone that frightened her.

No one answered. She now recognized some of the others: Mr. Gomez, Mrs. Limón, Maria Martinez, her young son, Fernando, Rebekah's neighbors Betty and Jeb, and Juanito, the caseworker she had let go. Some of them wore fatigues.

"What the?" said Rebekah, her voice shaking. "I expected to find USDA boxes of milk and butter. Not the Michigan Militia!" She let out a small, nervous laugh.

"Nelson Roy all but picked their pockets," Carlos smiled, indicating his fellow workers. "We're buying them pants."

"And then some," Rebekah said. "Mr. Roy said our old computers might be here. Now I get it. Missing files. Unauthorized benefits." Dávila laughed, and for the first time the wrinkles around his eyes that once had appeared to her so worldly and magnetic, so charmingly defiant, now in fact made him look old and corrupt.

"Yes, the farmworkers are very much into hacking!" he said. "Weeds. It's hard work, without benefits."

"And those mysterious government checks clearing some bank in Matamoros? Jesus, Carlos, what were you thinking?" She spoke sharply, and loathed the timbre of her own voice. Academic, clinical.

"I have nothing to do with any of that," said Carlos, moving toward her. "You must believe me."

"I want to."

"We sell your old hardware. Nothing more. The money goes to families that Roy cut off." He reached out to touch her. "We're not robbing banks." Now his tenderness had returned. That voice she'd leaned into, that voice she'd needed for selfish reasons—she now realized—as much as anything else.

"Maybe not," she said, "but there's principles." She remembered their first meeting. How Carlos had talked about the distribution of wealth in the country, institutional biases, and in the same breath, reparations for migrant farmworkers. It was her best vision of the world, the way it was supposed to be. Passion, an understanding of systems, a willingness to walk the talk. Touching him, she could touch *that*; the Stillwater River flowed into Lake Michigan and the Rio Grande into the Gulf of Mexico, and this man had a foot in each. He was electric. They had laughed together, drove the county fields and orchards together, and later, slept together. But she had never imagined this.

"No one says a thing when the farmers get relief after a drought, do they?" Carlos scoffed. "The government even pays them not to grow crops. Do they pay us not to eat? Principles are what gringos shout when they lose money."

"You're a fraud!" she railed at him. But Rebekah knew she might as well have been speaking to herself. Trying to fit in. Thinking she was someone different, and part of the migrants' lives. She looked at them, watching her and Carlos, decent people who had toiled in the fields all their lives. She'd been a student most of hers, dipping graham crackers into warm milk and watching sitcoms with her overweight dog. Then an English major. Grad school.

The chill and dampness of the room no longer made her shudder; she was, in part, numb.

Rebekah looked at the crease of daylight beneath the door at the top of the stairs. She wanted to run into the blistering sun to examine what she had been blind to: her lover's dark business; her own darkness, too. She started up the stairs.

"What will you do?" Carlos asked.

"I haven't decided." Nelson Roy had said to call as soon as she knew something. "I was on my way to my grandmother's. She's in a nursing home and not doing well. At least, that's what I had planned." She knew too that she'd pass the state police post at the edge of town. "Or should I look over my shoulder for the big bad wolf?"

"I would never hurt you."

"You already did."

They stood in the semi-darkness, she one step above him and looking squarely in his eyes. The color of blackened steak, she thought. And still on fire, one that she had been unwilling to run from. Or unable. Again, she started up the stairs. Carlos put a hand on her shoulder.

"Your grandmother," he said. "She's cared for by strangers?"

"Is your revolution going to fix that, too?"

"My revolution is about truth."

"Then the truth is, it's over."

Brave words, Rebekah thought as she walked out the door and got into her car, mired in self-doubt.

It was a long drive to see her grandmother and mother, Golda, but there was little traffic. A tease of golds and reds streaked the treetops. An hour out, she stopped for gas, called Carlos from the payphone, then hung up on his answering machine. She wasn't sure what she'd say, if he had answered. Mostly she wanted him to acknowledge the position his actions had put her in. Did he expect her to be a cheerleader and camp follower of his schemes, until, poco a poco, her heart and career both withered? Until she was let go for conduct "unbecoming of a state employee"? She remembered the oath she had signed in spring. Things were about to bloom then; there was promise. Her mind raced on, the car sped along, and the leaves in the now sparse woods were no longer turning colors.

Rebekah called Nelson Roy at a rest area outside Lansing. She said that she had nothing to do with Dávila and the computers. It was news to her as well. She wasn't even sure whose they were. He wasn't keeping the money, if he was selling them, she said, before hanging up. Maybe she should transfer downstate, as her mother had practically begged her to, she thought. She imagined the reference Roy might give her: *a bitch of a hard worker sleeping with a Mexican thug.* She had refused to have drinks with him more than once. Refused to step on his boat. Even so, the need for child welfare specialists was high; it was, sadly, a robust business.

Merging onto the freeway, Rebekah pictured herself living downstate. She would miss the lake and jogging past the farms and orchards where she'd see the Mexicans at work. Miss, too, seeing Carlos there, loading the day's bounty onto a flatbed truck, or talking to a farmer. He had never lied to her before, she thought, and she believed him now. The distance between Stillwater and Detroit had given Rebekah strength, a newness and vigor, and at times the confidence to push back against the whispering self that said she was a mere pretender. Along that road, she felt suspended between two cultures as well, seduced by one, too familiar with the other. *You can't ever go home again,* she thought and laughed out loud.

She'd last seen Golda on Mother's Day and had told her over lunch that she was falling in love. Golda half-smiled. Rebekah wanted that to be the end to her mother saying that she'd never meet anyone up there. As if *up there* was Siberia. And it worked. Then. She said her boyfriend's full name, slowly pronouncing each syllable. *Car-los. Dá-vi-la.* End of conversation. She truly was up there. Far away.

***

A handful of residents and visitors occupied the nursing home lobby, while small children ran about tossing bright coins into the fountain. Rebekah waited at the front desk for the receptionist. "I'm here to see my grandmother, Anna Katz," she said to a heavy-set Black woman of about fifty. Her name tag said Rosie.

"Anna darling!" Rosie shouted to a woman seated by the door. "You have a visitor."

Rebekah turned. "Oh! I walked right past her," she said, then hesitated. "When I talked to my mom, she said I was supposed to ask you for a book? A booklet or something."

Rosie handed Rebekah an application for public assistance. Rebekah started to say something, then looked away. Her heart skipped a beat. "Is something wrong?" the receptionist asked.

"No. I don't know," said Rebekah. "I thought my mother meant something else."

"When people say *book* here, they usually mean that. Your mother wants to apply for Medicaid for your grandmother."

"Yes," said Rebekah softly. "Pages six to nine, columns A through H." She knew each page of the application, and each was the story of someone's life—someone else's; the entries were not supposed to be hers. Her family didn't apply for assistance. She was certain there had been a misunderstanding.

"The social worker will be in Monday," said Rosie. "If you or your mother have any questions."

122

Rebekah went to her grandmother and knelt alongside her. Anna was looking at everything and nothing from the oversized upholstered chair that she seemed a part of, her deeply lined face without expression. She had an inoperable tumor in her liver.

"Hello grandma. It's Rebekah." Then, louder: "Grandma. It's Rebekah. Golda's oldest."

"Rebekah? Are you married?"

"No, grandma."

"They steal from me here. Combs, jewelry."

"We put your jewelry away. My mother has it. Golda."

"Voo iz Golda? Vaws vawlt eer geh-Valwlt?"

"Eekh red nawr English, Grandma. Please talk in English."

"Forgive me. You went far away to study. To Spain, didn't you? But you don't speak Yiddish. So, my Golda is here?"

"No, not today. I'm on my way to see her." Rebekah puzzled over what to say next and apologized for not visiting sooner. Anna said that she didn't hear so well and had to put her head in the *telebishen* to see it. She then turned to Rebekah, her moist brown eyes disproportionately large, even haunting, behind the thick lens of her glasses. "How old am I?"

Rebekah chuckled at the childlike innocence of the question. "Do you remember? I wrote a paper on you in college. You were born in Poland the same year 'America the Beautiful' was written on a mountain top in Colorado."

"Is it beautiful today?"

"You came to New York when you were nineteen and worked in a sweatshop in the garment district. When you had earned enough money, you sent for your brother Sam, then Nettie."

Anna wiped her lips with the back of her hand and cleared her throat. "Six dollars a week they paid me. I was the best."

"We're all damn immigrants, aren't we grandma?" said Rebekah. The sun streamed through the floor-to-ceiling windows and for a moment she watched the accidental rainbows that danced along the edge of the large petal-like fountain.

"I don't remember," said Anna, waving a frail hand then pressing herself deeper into the chair until only her white hair showed, curled and stiff like bales of straw.

Rebekah leaned over her. *"Bubbie,* when you moved in with us before you remarried, and we shared my bedroom…do you remember that? You slept so loud! I thought the paint would fall off the walls. I didn't know women snored. I was afraid that you were going to die in your sleep. I was so afraid." Anna raised her head. "I had bad dreams," Rebekah said. "And then I thought that if you did die, I'd have my room back all to myself." She squeezed the old woman's hands and could not hold back her tears. "I didn't want you to die, Anna. Not then. Not now."

"You were dating a nice boy. Richard. I knew his family."

"That was in high school. I finished graduate school, and I work now."

"Where?"

"In a small town up north. With one stoplight, one grocery and the closest synagogue forty miles away."

"How many are there?" said Anna.

The question confused Rebekah

"*Nu, iz yidn dortn?*"

"She wants to know if there are any Jews there," said Rosie from the front desk.

Rebekah didn't know any. She turned to the fountain where the afternoon sun from the high windows played tricks on the water, making it appear to flow in reverse. It made her stomach uneasy. The day had become like a dream to her, one that any minute she'd mercifully awake from as a better daughter, and granddaughter. A better employee. Rebekah looked at the application in her hands and wanted to tear it to shreds. She clutched the granola bar in her purse, realizing that she hadn't eaten since leaving her apartment. She yearned for the wide-open north, where she could climb the dunes above the lake barefooted and scream at the top of her lungs at the waves, and God.

The lobby turned quiet; the residents had retreated to their rooms, or the cafeteria. Anna slept in her chair, an afghan pulled to her chin. Rosie told Rebekah there was a call for her and directed her to a phone stand across the lobby. Rebekah, assuming it was her mother, picked up the phone and turned to where she could still observe Anna.

"Hello?"

"Carlos Dávila was arrested this afternoon," said Nelson Roy. "The church basement was like a damn flea market. And all of it from human services." There was a pause. Roy then asked, "Is there something you want to tell me?"

"Selling discarded computer equipment—wherever he obtained it—is not the same as hacking into the system and stealing thousands," said Rebekah.

"We'll see about that," Roy said. "Maybe Dávila had help from someone inside the agency. Someone he's close to."

"You can go to hell, Nelson."

She rejoined Anna and sat alongside her.

"Rebekah?"

"Yes, grandma."

"Your Uncle George put himself through law school carrying letters for the government. He delivered the mail to my shop in Hamtramck." Anna removed her glasses to wipe them on a dirty napkin she held crumpled in her hand. Rebekah thought that her runny eyes—unmasked, without magnification—overflowed with life, and yet were paradoxically vacant, too. "Are you well, daughter?" Anna said just then. "You seem bothered."

Rebekah sighed. "I have some tough decisions to make, grandma. And you frightened me a bit. Sleeping." She edged away to complete the application for assistance. Her hand was unsteady, the writing unlike anything she had ever done. She knew each question, and yet the words seemed to float above the page and she struggled to read them. Her heart pounded in her chest as if she had just completed a difficult run. She pretended to see her answers as if written by someone else, maybe an unemployed friend from grad school—how whimsical, that! Or a client.

Anna asked if she was doing homework. "You don't have to stay any longer, dear," she said.

Rebekah took the application to the front desk and waited. After some minutes, she left it there and joined Anna.

"Excuse me?" Rosie announced. Rebekah turned to see her holding the application by a corner. "You'll need to sign. Page—"

"Page twenty-six," said Rebekah. She signed, swallowed hard and then turned to the fountain where rainbows danced and the colors blurred.

***

The skies were clear when Rebekah left the nursing home for Golda's some twenty minutes away. There was road construction, however, and now, traffic. She thought hard how to avoid it. All of it. At the first stop light she could go north, then west towards Lake Michigan, and north again along the coast to Stillwater. Or she could turn right and take the highway to her mother's West Bloomfield townhouse. Her head was spinning, her car still. Stuck in traffic, she thought of what Carlos said to her the other week. She was passing Lakeshore Acres when she recognized Josefina, a young girl that her agency had approved as a childcare assistant. A handful of smaller children followed Josefina like ducklings as she darted in and out of the rows of vines. Rebekah parked the state car and confronted the girl's

125

father. Sweat streaked his dusty face, like war paint. "We pay Josefina to watch the children at the camp," Rebekah had said to him. "Not in the field." The mechanization dominating the pickle industry statewide had made few inroads into Bear County, where small hands made for easy pickings.

"As you can see, the camp is right there," the father scowled, motioning to a group of well-maintained trailers across the way. Under a makeshift canopy of bed sheets Rebekah saw a rocker, and the slight figure of an old woman moving rhythmically back and forth, like a metronome. Although they were the same height, she sensed the father looking down on her.

"And I see Josefina here, working," Rebekah said. The young girl then skipped back to the trailer with her siblings and cousins in tow. The crew resumed their labor and Rebekah started for her car. Behind her, the *tat-tat-tat* of cucumbers falling into buckets sounded like a gentle and mesmerizing rain.

"Harassing my crew?" From out of nowhere, Carlos was at her side, teasing her. The two walked past his tractor and toward shade.

"The field is no place for kids," she said. "The law says—"

"My first great lesson was in the field," he interrupted. "Picking cherries in Oregon. My father and uncles had crossed some invisible line in the orchard, and a white crew demanded all our lugs. They wanted a fight, and for the Mexicans to get thrown out. More work for them! I was ten, and I understood that. Not the oldest, but the only one who spoke English. I apologized for everything! The hot and dry weather, the shortage of ladders, the price of cherries. But we had work the next day. And the day after that."

Who was she, Rebekah now thought, to tell someone else rules and regulations? *Who was she* to chart right from wrong, black from white, ignoring the fucked-up gray in the middle where everyone just did what they could, trying their best not to be torn apart?

North or south? The light changed, and her mother waited.

***

Rebekah approached her mother's door with trepidation, touched the mezuzah on the jamb—more habit than prayer—and rang the buzzer. When there was no answer, she knocked loudly. The widow Golda, a retired schoolteacher and in good health, was always where she said she'd be. Always prompt. Reliable. When there still was no answer, Rebekah dug into the bottom of her purse, pulled out a key— and laughed. It had been a long time since she last used it, yet the key was there, like Kleenex, or lip gloss, a constant presence in one handbag or another. A relic from when she belonged, she thought, a realization that swept her laughter away. The key turned easily, and she opened the door. Golda stood in the foyer.

"Mother!" said Rebekah, alarmed. "Why didn't you let me in?"

"I...I really don't know," said Golda.

"I was worried that—"

"I'm sorry. It's such a silly thing," said Golda.

"What is?

"The key. I wanted to hear it turn in the door."

The women hugged, and with her mother's body pressed against her Rebekah realized that Golda, no longer chasing after first graders, had softened. The once angular hips were now rounded, the shoulders thicker, the neck less taut. Still, she was undeniably attractive. "I might have turned around and left," said Rebekah. "How did you know I'd have a key?"

"Because home meant something to you," Golda shrugged, and started towards the kitchen. She wore a designer warm-up suit that complimented long, strawberry blond hair which she had tied back, not a strand out of place. Her living room, too, was immaculate. A picture of a bride and groom—Golda with Rebekah's father—stood on a side table. A black and white portrait of Anna, Golda, Rebekah and her younger sister Judith with her infant son hung on a wall, framed by small and finely decorative mirrors from Golda's travels abroad. Only the baby was unsmiling.

"I heard you laugh," Golda said. Then added, "I don't think you looked for it long. The key, I mean." She offered her daughter some leftovers, and they sat. "You've lost weight. Did your grandmother recognize you? Are you eating?"

"Yes, mother. I've been running."

They talked about how it used to be, and the trip the three of them had made to New York only summers ago. Mother and daughter rarely allowed the other to finish a sentence.

"Your grandmother had such strength. Such resolve," Golda said, stifling a sob. "Did she ask anything about your work? She's so proud."

"The less, the better."

"Oh! Did Mr. Roy reach you? He said it was urgent."

"We talked," Rebekah said.

"I don't know why you went there. So far away from what you know."

"Caring isn't a matter of geography," said Rebekah.

"But we care most for what's closest," said Golda. "It's nature's way." The words struck Rebekah like a punch in the gut; for all her mother's meandering, she cut to the chase with indeliberate and disarming ease. "I would think there's little opportunity for advancement up north," Golda went on. "To have a good career. To meet someone and—"

"You mean someone Jewish!" said Rebekah.

"I never know what to say to you," said Golda.

"The receptionist at the Home gave me the application."

"Is that why you're so upset?"

"If you wanted me to pick up a damn application for public assistance, why didn't you just say so! You called it something else all summer, a *pamphlet* or *book*."

"But that's what they told me to ask for! I knew you were more familiar with those sorts of things and would do a better job completing it."

"You're right, mother. I see these applications every day. Generally, from people who have little. Or nothing."

"Maybe they want to save what's left."

"Mother—Grandma applying for Medicaid! What about her property? We are not a family who applies for welfare!"

"She has nothing."

"Now, but she did!"

"Would you have preferred to go to Wayne State instead of Brandeis? I didn't hear you complain then." Golda started to clear the table. "It's perfectly legal. Your aunt and I converted her assets years ago. For the grandchildren."

"So the government can pay her long-term care."

"So the family isn't left homeless, and you and your cousins have something to start your lives with!" Golda stood at her daughter's side, wringing her hands. "What am I guilty of? That I, a mother of moderate means, love my children and put their needs above the state?"

Rebekah thought this over, and got to her feet.

"Where are you going?" said Golda.

"To my office. I'm sorry."

"The office?" said Golda. "Your office is across the state. You just got here."

"You made me think of something," Rebekah said. "Something good."

"What did I do so good that it inspires you to leave?"

"You said that we care most for what's closest."

Golda turned away from Rebekah to look out the kitchen window. Her shoulders slumped. "I made your room up. I haven't seen you all summer. The Holy Day starts tomorrow at sundown. Did you forget?"

"I'll call when I get there."

"Is it trouble with Mr. Dav-ilo?"

"Yes. Trouble with Mr. Dávila," said Rebekah. She embraced Golda, then pushed her gently away.

***

Approaching Bear County hours later, Rebekah saw wisps of black smoke rising, and within a few miles passed an orchard where in the center small piles of brush burned. She thought of her career going up in smoke as well. What then? Pick apples with Dávila and his crew? She smiled at the thought, and the emotion surprised her. She turned her car into a picnic area along Lake Michigan, which was as smooth as glass as far as she could see. The setting sun was easy on her eyes, and she watched the last of it slip into the water. Rebekah then walked across the two-lane where at the edge of a field she saw the fat pickles too large to harvest, crimson and orange in the fading light, half-plowed under in the loose soil and left to rot.

Two Poems

by Jeremy Jusek

Jeremy Jusek is Parma's poet laureate. He authored two collections, We Grow Tomatoes in Tiny Towns *(2019) and* The Less Traveled Street *(2022). He hosts the Ohio Poetry Association's podcast Poetry Spotlight, runs the West Side Poetry Workshop, and founded the Flamingo Writers Guild. To learn more, visit Jeremyjusek.com.*

EXT. OUTSIDE CENTURY 3 MALL – NIGHT, OCTOBER

Two young rebellious deer heroines
after a wild night out
    prancing among the dilapidated monument to middle class capitalism
    not content with the rough turf buffet outside the former JC Penny lot
Daisy and Delilah venture
to the Pep-Boys dandelions
    tragedy lurks
    and thy name is white wrangler
jamming to the Grateful Dead
Pete is once again blindsided by wildlife
    Daisy hops, stumbles, escapes
    Delilah hears her mother's voice:
"They always hit the second one!"
Today the ancient deer folklore rings true.
Pete heartlessly screams "break a leg!"
But the deer's performance is done—
Fortune shines through the LEDs, its spotlight
cast along the mall's brick. Delilah bows her encore
    hops the divide, destined to dutifully
    despoil suburban gardens once again.

SCENE

NOTE: Co-written with Tyler Stay

Alzheimer's Birds

My grandmother offered comfort:
        a comforter to each grandchild
        for finishing high school.

A series of roses tangled together
Dominate the central white spread,
muted baby blues harboring doves
assuredly birds that love for life.
        the album was wrapped in red and orange leaves,
        her then falling aside to our now

As I settle into evening, a bird-laden bough
        waterfalls less than three feet,
their gibbering beaks sealed in eternal conversation,
unaware that they spill downward into blackness.
        Or that, you know, they're trapped
in the second dimension, unable to grow up.
        The floorboards and slippers
        greet the downy bird song
        with a gentle fuzzy nuzzle.

I focus on
        The adjustable event horizon beneath my chin.
        The real bird song outside my window.
        The strange wheezing of the new fridge.
        The word "the" as an articulating article.

And how scary it is to consider the temporary nature of a family unit,
and the inevitable shred
        time mandates upon our precious thing—

But my blanket bird family is locked in song as long as I care for it
        slowly stretching and wearing thin
        yet always as I remember it
            hardly daring to change.

When the blanket is tugged backward,
stitched roses slink into view,
many others off the edge

into a place that frays
at the edge of memory.

The kind of place the TV remote goes
            when it's feeling depressed.
And when it returns
            it tells me how yet again
                    my grandmother is mute
                            and shedding leaves.

Danny

by Leon Taylor

Leon teaches economics at KIMEP University in Almaty, Kazakhstan, a post-Soviet nation in Central Asia. A Hoosier, Leon was a newspaper reporter in Lexington, KY and Evansville, IN and a magazine writer for Cincinnati Magazine, before becoming an economist. He's written fiction for Schlock!, Space and Time, 96th of October, 365tomorrows, kaidankai, Sanitarium, Mono blog, Spotlong Review, The Quiet Reader, The Unpleasantville Anthology, *and other publications.*

I turned 16 in the summer when my best friend died, and I doubted that I would see 17. When you are 16, you know that you will live forever, but any evidence to the contrary destroys your certitude. You gradually realize that death is just around the corner.

But before Danny drowned, if he drowned, I thought that I had all the time in the world. I spent most of it growing a mustache—to the indignation of my father, who was pure ethnic Irish, pure Hoosier, and a coal miner's son. I didn't care. *Butch Cassidy and the Sundance Kid* was playing on the outdoor film screens. Mustaches were in, and fathers were out.

For early teens in Brownsburg, Indiana, population 11,000, the outdoor theater on the shabby edge of town, the Stardust, was our cultural epicenter. It was proof of manhood, because you had to be 16 to drive, or at least a surreptitious 15. Boys with wheels were popular with the girls, but it was not clear what you should do after parking in the back row. I idolized my brother, who was 23 and played be-bop on alto saxophone when he wasn't racing jalopies. So, I listened closely when he advised me on how to behave on my first date. "Don't make out. Watch the film. I always get furthest when I play hard to get." Only when I turned 23 did I realize that my brother was just bragging to his biggest fan. Anyway, my date, the lissome Cheri, was more interested in real life than in celluloid, so she left me in the back seat of the family Valiant and climbed into the front seat of a spanking new Chevy, driven by my future ex-next-best friend.

Since I was not destined to become a gigolo, I needed another teen career. I chose running. Cross-country and track appeal to cowards like me who prefer to stay out of harm's way (i.e., the gridiron). And the rules and techniques are simpler than in basketball. My best friend, Danny, had long razzed me for my push-shot. This did not stop me from playing pickup during the lunch hour, just before our civics class, or trying out for the middle-school team. But with my height of 5'3" and my mile-high dribble, I was fated for the first cut.

Cross-country was another matter. It was a sport for masochists, and I did not mind the rising pain that preceded second wind. Danny, on the other hand, was gangly and awkward on the track, stepping too high to run miles efficiently. But he was balletic on the basketball court. So we exercised together, coaching one another. To improve our practice shots, Danny slightly deflated the basketball so that it would not go through the basket on a lucky bounce. Only perfect shots counted. Most of them were Danny's, as he was careful to point out. He was tall and black-haired, with Woody Allen glasses, a cornpone sense of humor, and a ready guffaw.

To shape up for cross-country, Danny ran daily to the White River and swam for a quarter mile. He was skillful in water and earned his pocket pay in the summer as a lifeguard at Brownsburg's only public swimming pool. I didn't accompany him on his runs to the river because I had never progressed past the dog paddle. So Danny exercised with a friend of ours, Reginald. Nervous and nervy, Reginald lived in Peyton, 20 miles from Brownsburg. He drove to the White River every few days to see a mysterious someone and row her across the stream to a secluded wood filled, regrettably for the barely-appareled, with poison ivy. From Brownsburg, Reginald wobble-biked to the river while Danny jogged and complained about the dirt-road drivers playing Chicken, a la James Dean. Then Danny swam while Reginald rowed across the placid White in his peeling boat, where he was an easy target for the bombarding robins above.

"Danny, why are you doing this?" I once asked. "Brownsburg doesn't even have a swimming team."

He blushed. "Don't tell anyone. I'm going to try out for the Olympics Triathlon."

One day, Danny didn't show up for our afternoon pickup game. I found the reason on Page One of the afternoon paper. He had drowned in two feet of water. "Baloney," my brother said, lighting up a Marlboro. "Reginald killed him in a fight over Amanda." A junior varsity cheerleader, with flaxen braids and sparkling blue eyes. "Clobbered him over the head with the oar."

"Reginald wouldn't do that," I said. "This is Brownsburg, Indiana. People here don't kill each other." My brother smiled and snuffed his cigarette. He always kept a spare pack in the sleeve of his T-shirt, rolled up to show off his auto mechanic's bicep.

I hadn't even known that Danny had a girlfriend. At that age, I was consumed by sports, the ticket to glory in a small Indiana town. I proposed that the cross-country team attend the funeral in our running suits. Instead, the coach, Gordon Smith, known to the team as Gordo for his girth, awarded Danny a junior varsity jacket of deep purple and light blue. Behind him was Danny in his casket, yellowish and slightly bloated, dressed in a suit that he would have hated.

For the rest of the week, not an hour passed that I did not think of Danny. I did not laugh when the class wit said we should put his photo for the yearbook in a glass of water. And I couldn't help dwelling on the feverish vision of Danny as a ghost. But it was Indian summer. The leaves were turning from green to scarlet and scorching yellow, and the temperature was diving into the sixties, delicious for running. Death lost its grip on my mind. It is hard to hold in prospect the fresh-dug grave when the weather has you kicking up your heels.

We were practicing for the sectional track meet in Brownsburg, a tournament of the middle and high schools in hilly southern Indiana. Normally the races were dominated by Peyton, which had a population of 20,000 and therefore looked down its nose at Brownsburg. Coach Huckleberry, deep-voiced and drawling, assigned me to the mile relay, in which each of four runners completes a quarter mile and passes the baton to the next runner. There are not many sophisticated techniques in running, but passing the baton is one of them. The receiving runner must take the baton within a 7-foot length of track. Both runners must coordinate the handoff so that they are simultaneously running at peak speed. Mike and I practiced endlessly, to the point that I did not even look at Mike during the handoff, just at his open hand.

The night of the meet was warm and moonlit. A brass band blared the fight song out of tune, with crowds huzzaing. The intoxicating smell of mown grass around the pole vault area mingled with the pungent aroma of chemicals sprayed on the track to ensure the spring of the soft asphalt. Spotlights illuminated the start line.

The first leg of a mile relay excites a crowd almost as much as does Churchill Downs. The lap takes less than a minute to complete, so fans with an attention-deficit syndrome don't have to strain themselves. And our lead runner, Bill, was popular throughout the high school for his mustache. He drew resounding cheers after the start gun fired. And he was fired up himself, bursting into a one-yard lead, until he pulled a thigh muscle on the back stretch. He fell behind Peyton and Rockford, and the crowd fell quiet as he handed off in a near-walk, shaking his head and cursing himself.

Normally, that would have been the end of the race. A bungled handoff wastes precious seconds. But George, our second runner, was angry, either at Bill or Fate. And a runner instinctively works off anger by dashing. And Peyton and Rockford were in the worst position of a race—the lead because you can't see how the contest is shaping up. Looking back would knock you off your stride. You can only look ahead and pray. And the prayer is insincere, because a runner who is yards in the lead in such a short race can't help but relax. By the time that Peyton and Rockford realized what was happening, they had lost the lead. Discouraged, Rockford fell behind. George and Peyton were neck-to-neck when my leg began.

I was the weakest runner on the relay team, which was why I ran third; the fourth runner, normally the strongest on the team, makes up for his predecessor's dalliance. But this was the *sectional*, so I was brimming with vim. It was only 440 yards, I told myself, and I could recover over the weekend while catching up on the Kentucky sports in the *Louisville Courier-Journal.* Plus, I didn't want to look worse than George. I sprinted to the point of fainting, blindly handing off to Mike in a dead heat.

Breathing easily, Mike took long graceful strides. He was such a blur of speed that I couldn't make out his face as he rounded the track, one, two, three yards in the lead. But this was not a done deal. His Peyton rival was our erstwhile friend Reginald, short, barrel-chested, and unshaven, like a thug. He was known for sidling up behind the rival in the home stretch and spiking his ankles. (Track shoes have spikes for traction.) Moreover, Mike tended to fade in the last 50 yards. His usual strategy was to build up a lead in the middle stretch that would discourage a challenge. But a shrewd runner like Reginald would anticipate this ploy and simply wait to accelerate in the home stretch when Mike would be on his last legs.

Sure enough, in the last 100 yards, Reginald revved up, leaned in, and stomped on Mike's right foot. But Mike didn't even react. It was as if the spikes met pure air.

But this, with 50 yards to go, was only a temporary setback for Peyton, we knew. We glumly waited for Mike's famous choke. Suddenly Mike kicked in with a third wind, gripping the baton like a weapon. He finished the race two yards ahead of wheezing, disconsolate Reginald, with a personal best of 51 seconds.

The Brownsburg folks in the stands erupted and mobbed the track. But Mike was nowhere to be found.

"Who ran that last leg?" said Huckleberry.

"Mike, of course."

"Mike didn't show up tonight. Measles."

We walked to the endfield, which was the touchdown zone in football season, where our last runner had taken off his sweats and warmed up in the far corner. In the wind-bent weeds, we found a new junior-varsity jacket and a slightly deflated basketball.

Two Poems
by Damian Ward Hey

Damian Ward Hey is published in The RavensPerch, e·ratio, Neologism, Trouvaille Review, Trailer Park Quarterly, *and in numerous other journals. His poems have also appeared in several anthologies, among them* Birth - Lifespan Vol. 1. *(Pure Slush),* Poets with Masks On *(Finishing Line), and* easing the edges: a collection of everyday miracles *(d. ellis phelps, ed.). He has a BA in English from Columbia University, a Ph.D. in Comparative Literature from Stony Brook University, and is the founding editor of Stone Poetry Journal. Damian is a professor of literature at Molloy University on Long Island, NY, where he lives with his wife and two children.*

American Twilight

Bird of moon, flow
deeply through the river
as cattle converse,

as travelers
build lives of odds and ends
along the broken road.

Somewhere, near,
wild stories are re-tamed
as coffee pours —

though window-light,
alone, across a solemn field,
is not always a beacon,

somewhere, still,
a stoic farmer may look out
and dream.

Cameo

I claw a cameo from life
And stab it to my chest.

I scrawl a triolet for death
And chuck it to the road

I shout out loud to far-off friends
And gamble I'll get there

I gasp in time when time is young
And hanging from the stars

I pay no mind to any turn
But drive my spirit raw

I look upon myself, at last
My face a battered grin

I crash my body in a ditch
Without an end in sight.

Travel Light

(previously published by Penduline Press, 2013)

by Paul Lamb

Paul Lamb lives near Kansas City but escapes to his Ozark cabin whenever he gets the chance. His novel, One-Match Fire, *is forthcoming from Blue Cedar Press and his short stories have appeared in dozens of literary journals. He rarely strays far from his laptop.*

Dusk was falling when Chris caught them. The miserable day was nearly done. Last to arrive, he was bone tired and wanted to sleep, but he wanted dinner more. He'd seen the twinkle of their campfire long before he reached the island, his canoe grinding on a final hidden sandbar; he had to clamber out and drag it the last hundred feet through ankle-deep water. His feet sank in the muddy sand, his sneakers filled with it, but he no longer cared. He just wrenched each foot from the sucking bottom and plodded forward, finally dragging his canoe onto the island, then throwing himself down in the gathering dark, on dry ground again.

Snatches of their chatter drifted to him. His shoulder muscles, his arms screamed. He never wanted to rise from his heap on the edge of the island, but he had to pitch his tent while there was still light. And he was starving.

"I've never been on an adventure like this," Martha had said with the innocent sparkle that popped into her words sometimes. Huddled at the put-in point that morning, hands deep in pockets and arms held close to their sides as they tried to ignore the chill. A day on the water daunting and possibly unpleasant to most of them; it had sounded more fun around the office conference table. The paved road they'd come down had given way to gravel and finally to dirt that disappeared into the river before them. The battered metal canoes were lined up and packed with their gear. Mackie and Eric were the last to arrive, as expected, so the group didn't get on the water as soon as Danny had hoped.

Danny, perpetually upbeat, looked at his watch as they waited. He'd volunteered to organize the trip since he'd suggested it. That was Chris' first staff meeting as supervisor. No one was sure of their changed relationships, and he thought the meeting had come off surprisingly not terrible. Even Mackie kept himself under control, though nobody expected that to last. Corporate said it would pay for monthly team building, in part to ease the transition of the new boss, and when Chris reached that point on his agenda, Danny spoke first. Chris hadn't been floating since he was in Scouts a decade before. Those had been on fast-running Ozark streams, not the sluggish, muddy Kaw. But the Kaw River was close to the city; everyone could manage it. And when Danny suggested camping overnight on a sandbar–he'd done it many times himself–he was so caught up that no one wanted to deflate his enthusiasm. And so, the department found itself waiting on the riverbank that Saturday morning, ready to begin but unable to start, looking to Chris for direction. He quickly deferred to Danny who actually knew what he was doing.

Danny had lined up their equipment beside the road: the tents, the coolers of food and beer, all their personal things mostly in trash bags. He parceled it out so no one's canoe would be weighed down with too much. And though everyone had already paired up for partners, Misty made a last-minute, giggling defection to ride with Willy and Pete. So, Danny shifted some of their gear into Chris' canoe since he no longer had a partner.

Chris knew what was going on. Misty would certainly have more fun with Willy and Pete, but what was left unspoken was that without her, his canoe wouldn't ride as low in the water. It was already going to carry the weight of two with just him. Everyone was polite enough not to discuss the purpose of the new arrangement, and about then Mackie and Eric had arrived, so they were finally ready to get underway.

Danny waded into the water, holding his canoe steady while Martha stepped into the bow gingerly, her natural caution mixed with genuine excitement. The others launched behind Danny, their new leader for the weekend, but when Chris plopped into his canoe and attempted his first stroke, his paddle scraped across the sandy bottom and his canoe did not move.

"Try to stay in the channel everyone," Danny shouted from ahead. "The water is deeper there." Chris watched as the other canoes drifted away. He sat mired on the bottom, and he tried to urge his canoe ahead by pushing his paddle into the sand and leaning on it. Inches. Finally, he stepped out and walked his canoe into deeper water, the first of many times. By then the others were already strung out ahead. He could see their canoes dancing through the eastern light glinting off the water.

Now Chris lay in the sand. He didn't want to get up, ever, but his stomach growled, and there was still his tent to pitch. So, with his screaming muscles he pushed himself from the yielding sand and sought the tent he had lashed in his canoe. Long years had passed since he'd used the tent, but he managed to pitch it in the gathering dark without much trouble. Far from the others so his snoring wouldn't keep them awake. He didn't need *that* added to the department fodder.

He didn't know what else he had carried in his canoe–Danny had given careful thought to what he shifted when Misty defected–but it didn't look as though they needed any of it just then. No one had hurried over to fetch anything when he arrived. Among the various bags he'd carried was another tent; someone was going to need that soon, but they could find it themselves. He staggered back to his canoe, his feet twisting in the island sand, and grabbed a couple of the dry bags to carry over to the fire. Martha was suddenly at his side.

"I came as quickly as I could. Let me help." She took one of the bags then led him to the fire. Up the river to the west the sun was setting with last shreds of a purple blaze, but Chris was too tired to notice, and the rest of them were too far along to care. Someone knocked down the towering fire; a shower of orange sparks rose into the night. Silhouettes of people before the flames. The smell of wood smoke.

"Didn't think you could miss us if I made the fire big enough," Mackie said, holding a piece of driftwood in one hand and a beer in the other. Chris dumped the bag he was carrying next to the others.

"Careful," said Danny. "Our breakfast is in there." But he didn't sound too worried.

A few of them were sitting in folding chairs. Where had they packed those? One of them would probably get up and offer him a chair, but he knew that if he sat in it, the feet would sink deep in the sand and he'd look ridiculous; probably topple out of it. Better to get seated on his own and avoid that whole awkward situation. He'd have to sit cross legged in the sand, if he could manage it, and his legs would fall asleep, but he didn't want to get up once he was down, and he didn't care anymore. He was tired. He was hungry. His shoulders hurt. His hips hurt. He wanted a beer. The first day was finally over. One more day and the trip would be over. He was not having fun.

At the edge of the firelight, he saw the coolers lined up, and he eased over. Inside he found a few cans of pop and many cans of beer sloshing around in the remains of the ice. Grabbing his second beer of the day, Chris realized that if he dragged the cooler closer to the fire, he could sit on it. A solid seat with a broad base. Perfect. He could sit down and never get up, except to get more beer. He'd been sitting in an unsteady canoe all day, but he was constantly pushing himself out of it to drag the canoe into deeper water. It was time to sit and not get up for a while. He'd earned it.

Kim and Martha sat across from him, sharing quiet words. Martha held a beer in her hand. So, alcohol did pass her lips. The angel of their office. Had she ever done anything to be ashamed of? Could anyone really be so good?

Beyond the firelight he could hear Misty giggling. "You are so bad!" she squealed, and he guessed she was speaking to Willy or Pete. Probably both. Chris pulled on his beer and felt his aching muscles begin to relax. A few more beers and a promised steak and maybe the insults of at least one day would drift away.

"Looks like the coals are ready," Danny said as he poked the fire with a piece of driftwood. "Time to put the steaks on."

Mackie brought over the grill and balanced it between a big log and the pile of rocks Danny had arranged. Rocks on a sandbar? Where had those come from? Chris figured he should probably know about such things, but his outdoor adventures were just memories, selectively tinted with the golden light of his youth. He dropped his empty on the sand and rose from the cooler to get another beer.

A dozen steaks sizzled on the grill. Everyone was gathered around the fire. A few flashlights were trained on the steaks, but it was hardly necessary. Once they were sufficiently cooked, they would be pulled from the grill and devoured. And then more would be laid on. Plenty for everyone. A bag of chips was passing around, but when it reached Chris, it was mostly crumbs. He held the bag to his mouth and tilted his head back, pouring it in. Some of it went down his shirt.

He closed his eyes and felt the exhaustion of the day mingle with the mellowing of the beer. The fire toasted his face and the front of his legs. Voices murmured and coals hissed, but he wasn't listening. He smelled smoke and cooking meat and always the wet, fecund smell of the river. Once or twice the beam of a flashlight swiped across his face, but all anyone saw was what looked like a contented smile. The beer was doing its job, taking him out of himself for a while.

By the second bend in the river that morning, Chris felt the first twinges in his shoulders, and he gave up any hope of keeping up. They had drifted ahead, staying in the current without effort, while he struggled for every inch. It seemed like that. When he did find the channel in the murky flow, when he thought he might make some time and get closer to them, he still had to paddle constantly. It was always work to keep moving forward. Everyone else made it look easy. Why did he always have to struggle? Danny could read the river. He knew how to work it to his advantage. But Mackie and Eric? How did they manage it? "Remember, everyone," Danny had shouted when they started. "It's not a race. There's no prize for getting there first." Soon all Chris heard were snippets of laughter that drifted upstream, their canoes just colorful dots on the water far ahead.

Chris had two large pockets in the vest he wore. He'd packed them with Milky Way bars: a half dozen for each day. Snacks and a little quick energy from the sugar. He needed to stop eating that way, he knew that, but a weekend float trip was no time to begin.

After an hour he'd lost sight of them altogether. He was a seasoned canoeist, not as much as Danny obviously, but experienced with a paddle. He assumed that was why they left him behind. That and the inevitable way people just drifted along, mostly heedless of anyone else.

"There's Chris!" Misty shouted when he had come around a bend midway through the morning. The other canoes were pulled onto a sandy beach. They had waited for him to catch up. He saw a few beer cans and a chip bag on the ground among them, and he watched Willy pour a half bag of chips onto the sand and then crumple the bag and drop it. As he drifted up to the beach, the others were already getting into their canoes and pushing off. Waiting for him to catch up did not include waiting for him to rest up. He had his bottles of water, and he still had two of his Saturday candy bars left, but he wanted some greasy chips, and he figured it wasn't too early in the day for at least one beer. But off they went, with all the snacks and beer in their canoes. He wondered if that was part of Danny's thoughtful rearrangement of the gear.

Lunch wasn't much better. By the time he reached the sandbar where they had pulled out, the gang had eaten most of the sandwiches. They'd left only one for him, which he ate in three bites, and a greasy napkin holding some Doritos. They had one beer for him, already warm from waiting on the sand.

The outfitter had described the approach to the island for their overnight, but no one was exactly sure where it was. Even Danny admitted he wasn't certain since the features of the river changed so much. Thus, Mackie and Eric volunteered to go ahead and find it. Soon Misty, Willy, and Pete had their canoe in the water too. Chris begged them to linger a bit so he could rest, but off the two canoes went. He lay in the sand, staring at the empty blue sky, never wanting to rise again. He heard the snap of a trash bag being opened. Someone was cleaning up. Chris figured he should help, so he rolled onto his stomach then pushed himself up. He stumbled across the soft sand to where Danny was. On the way he bent to grab a napkin, but the breeze sent it tumbling toward the water. He didn't chase it.

But that day was done, and he sat on his cooler before the fire, gorging on the smell of the steaks cooking. They would burn but he didn't care. He would devour his and gnaw on the bone to get every crispy ounce of gristle and fat. When he opened his eyes, he saw Martha stabbing a steak from the grill and sliding it onto a plate. He could have crowded up with the rest of them and gotten himself a half-raw, half-burnt steak right away, but he knew that was no behavior for a fat man. Despite his hunger, his exhaustion, despite all the beer in him, he still kept some dignity.

Someone passed between him and the fire; he felt sudden coolness sweep over him. It was Martha, holding a plate with the cooked steak before him.

"I don't want you to think I'm trying to curry favor with the boss," she whispered. "But you looked so tired."

Had she really brought him the first steak off the grill? He screwed his beer into the sand and accepted the plate. She gave him a napkin and a half-full bag of chips.

"Hardly the boss," he said, delirious from the smell of the meat. "I just check your reports and pass them up line."

Even if she weren't already married with two little boys, Martha was out of his league. She was maybe his age, but she was a pixie. Her husband took her to Royals games and the ballet. She sent Chris postcards from places like Malta and Barbados.

"Enjoy," she said. Maybe she smiled at him, but he couldn't tell in the darkness. All he could see was the nimbus of her short hair backlit by the fire.

The plastic knife and fork Martha had given him didn't work very well on the paper plate; he didn't have much lap to balance it on. Finally, he just took the steak in his hand and tore off a piece with his teeth, washed it down with a gulp of beer, then followed with a handful of chips. He finished his dinner in a couple of minutes, and he threw the bone into the darkness, hoping to hear it hit the water. But he had no arm and it fell short.

There would be more steaks than takers, he knew, but he wasn't going to get himself another in front of everyone. Rolled up with his dry clothes was a plastic box full of chocolate chip cookies. And he still had two of Sunday's Milky Ways left in his vest after a late, famished raid on them. He poured the last crumbs from the bag of chips into his mouth and opened another beer. Then he collected his trash and carried it over to the fire. The plate flared up, but the chip bag and plastic utensils just shriveled and smoked. He'd lost the napkin.

Kim stumbled through the group, handing out beers and veering close to the fire. Misty was somewhere beyond the firelight, laughing again. "Stop it!" she said, but it didn't sound like she meant it. Everyone was fed and mellow. Danny made an effort to pick up the empties and the other trash, but he couldn't see much beyond the ring of light from the fire, and he soon gave up. Danny had no trouble dropping cross-legged in the sand.

Chris pulled his cooler closer to the fire to be with the others. Their faces wavered in the flickering light, so different from the steady glare of the fluorescent lights at the office. He closed his eyes.

"This float trip was a great idea, Danny," Mackie said.

Chris figured he should have said that. He was supposed to be their boss.

Everyone agreed with Mackie. Danny bobbed his head in acknowledgement, and then they let a genial silence fall among them.

After a while, Danny said that if no one was going to eat the remaining steaks, they'd have to throw them in the river. Otherwise, they'd have raccoons visiting the camp that night.

"Then throw them in the river," said Martha.

No one got up to do it though. Tired and half drunk and comfortable, they all leaned back and let the silence enwrap them.

After a sufficient time, Chris pushed up from the cooler. "I'll do it."

There were five steaks left. They had been moved to the edge of the grill where they wouldn't burn, but even so, they felt dry and crispy. He stumbled through the sand toward where he thought the river was, and when he got past the tents and the ring of fire light, he began tearing bites from one of the steaks. His prize for coming in last. The edge was burned and crunched in his teeth, but he spit that first piece out and tried again, finding better meat in the center. By the time he got to the water, he had eaten as much of the first steak as he could find in the darkness and started on the second one. He ate all that he could from the five then threw the bones into the darkness, listening for their splash each time. He bent toward the water with a grunt and rinsed his hands, drying them on his pants, then he turned toward camp, using the fire has his beacon.

Still beyond the light himself, he could see several faces painted with the orange glow from the fire.

"Did you see how high his bow was above the water?" Mackie said.

"I started laughing when I looked back and saw it!" That was Eric. Chris wasn't surprised.

"I think he walked more miles than he floated."

"Stop it you two," said Martha. "You're drunk. Don't be so mean. Chris is a good person."

"Yeah, he's a good guy," Mackie conceded, and then they fell silent.

Chris let the quiet collect before he stumbled toward the fire.

"Hey, welcome back," said Mackie quickly. "What took you so long?"

"Too much beer." That raised a chuckle.

Before taking his seat on the cooler again, he opened it and pulled out a beer. "Anyone?"

A few hands raised, and he began tossing cans. Only Danny caught his. The others thudded into the sand, but they were opened without too much mess or complaint.

Another bag of chips made the rounds. Kim suggested making 'Smores, but no one had the energy to bother. The conversations dissolved to sporadic murmurings. A few more beers and Chris was ready for bed.

"How far to the takeout point tomorrow?"

"Not far. Less than five miles, I think," said Danny. "A couple hours."

"Well, I'm going to bed. See all of you in the morning. We'll skip our regular staff meeting."

That raised a laugh too, and with a last wave, he turned to find his tent. The flashlight he should have been carrying was rolled up with his dry clothes and the cookies. He knew he was close when he tripped over the extra gear he'd removed from his canoe. Someone hadn't set up their tent yet, and he was glad it wasn't him. They were all too drunk by then to manage something that complicated, especially in the dark.

He didn't want to climb into his tent wearing his sandy, wet sneakers, but he worried that if he left them outside, some animal would carry them off in the night, so he tumbled into the tent and zipped the door shut behind him. He'd clean it in the morning.

Taking off his dirty sneakers. Peeling off his wet socks. Drying his feet. Pulling on dry socks over his ragged toenails. All of this was nearly impossible for Chris because he could barely reach his feet as he sat on the tent floor, and after he managed each step, he fell onto his back and gasped for air. The sand beneath the tent yielded with each fall, and by the time he was finished, a crater formed where his head had struck.

He expected to have a bad night, and he struggle with his gear to make a nest. His doctor said he would sleep better if he just lost a hundred pounds. More like a hundred and fifty, Chris knew.

He pulled the sleeping bag over his shoulder and rolled on his side, hoping he was tired or drunk enough to fall asleep quickly. He tried not to remember the things they said about him around the fire. Things they were probably still saying.

He was the first to wake in the morning. Once he saw the first hint of dawn through the fabric of his tent, he figured his punishment was sufficiently over; a different punishment replaced it. His arms and shoulders ached. He could barely move his fingers. His hands were claws, and he never wanted to hold a paddle again. His head pounded, but that was normal, an old friend come for a visit.

As he moved, his muscles began to loosen, and by the time he pulled his sandy sneakers on, he thought he might make it through the morning.

Outside, no one else was awake. The campfire, farther away than he realized, sent a reluctant string of white smoke into the air. At his feet was what he had tripped over in the dark. Someone hadn't set up their tent after all, and before he could consider the implications of that, he knew he had to get something to eat.

He guessed one of the coolers had breakfast in it, but he didn't remember seeing anything when he had dug in them the night before. Plus, he was reluctant to raid the supplies and be caught stuffing his face with everyone else's food.

On the ground by the fire, he found a box of Graham crackers half eaten. Beside it was an open bag of marshmallows that were dusted with sand. If there had been any chocolate bars for the 'Smores they were all gone. Or maybe hidden in someone's tent.

A pair of crows passed silently over the island. Those early birds were out to get the worm, he guessed, and so was he. He took his same seat on the cooler. Then he picked up the box of Graham crackers and began shoving them in his mouth as fast as he could. When they were gone, he put the box on the coals, willing it to flare up and destroy the evidence. Then he took the marshmallows out of the bag one by one and dusted off the sand before popping each into his mouth. They were awful, but he was hungry. When he was finished, he twisted the marshmallow bag into a tight ball and shoved it deep in the sand. Danny wouldn't approve, but he didn't have to know. He rose from the cooler and opened it. After briefly considering a beer, he opened a can of pop and washed down his dry and sticky breakfast. That would hold him until his real breakfast, and he worried that would not be for a long time while everyone slept off their hangovers.

The sun was inching over the trees down river. Soon it would hit the tents, and maybe then some of them would stir.

He sat on the cooler and tried not to think about how much he hated his life. They all thought he was a nice guy, easy to get along with, not a difficult boss. He was amazed that nobody could see how miserable he was, how terrible everything really was. Every day, waking with a shriek of recognition. Every day another struggle. Every day the same struggle. He was the same man he had been the day before, and he had to live the same wretched life he had the day before. He worked. He paid his bills. He saved a little. Sometimes he went to the movies, but he hated going alone. He got carry out all the time, except when he had pizza delivered. Even so, his grocery bill was big enough for a family. He hated climbing the stairs to his second-floor apartment. He hated the way his seat belt barely reached the buckle and the steering wheel rubbed his stomach even with the seat back as far as he dared. He hated dropping anything on the floor because he could scarcely bend over enough to reach it. His knees were starting to hurt. His feet had always hurt. He hated all of those things, but he hated himself most of all. Something had to change, and nothing ever did.

He wiped his eyes then pushed himself up from the cooler. Maybe by the time he had his tent down and his gear stowed in his canoe, someone would have breakfast started. He walked to his tent, his ankles twisting in the sand. His life was no life.

It was when he had his tent down, rolled and ready to be slipped into its bag that he saw it. There, right where his tent had been, close to the canoes where everyone would be returning, was an impression of his bulk in the sand. Negative space showing just how much space he claimed, twice his share of the world. He could make out where his shoulder had pressed in, where his hips were, and a circular crater between them that was most of the rest of him. There was the truest summation his life for all of them to see.

He looked toward the other tents. No one was stirring. He fell to his knees with a thud and started scattering the sand with his hands. He pushed it around and dug deep holes where there weren't any before. He jabbed the sand with a piece of driftwood and pounded it with his fists, screaming silently all the while. And when he was done and had erased all sign of himself, he zipped open the pocket on his vest where he had his two remaining candy bars. He shoved them into one of the holes he had dug and covered them with sand.

Then he fell to his side, exhausted. "No more. I have to change!"

After a while, he pushed himself up from the sand and finished packing. He stowed the gear in his canoe but didn't tie it down because he knew he'd have other gear to carry.

Over at the fire he saw Danny poking the coals. Martha was working the tabs off the beer cans scattered around. Neither looked too happy to be alive, but at least they were finally up. Chris wandered over, trying not to seem eager.

"So, I figured if I could reduce everything by one quarter," Danny was saying to Martha, "my whole pack would weigh less. Look at each item and find a way to trim the weight. I cut half the handle off my toothbrush, for example. And that's how I travel light. By an accumulation of little things."

"Good morning, fearless leader," Martha said as Chris stumbled up.

Danny picked up one of the dry bags that Chris had carried in his canoe the day before. "Breakfast is ready."

From inside he pulled out several boxes of glazed donuts. How they had survived the journey without getting smashed Chris did not know. Danny opened the boxes and set them on the coolers beside the fire.

"There are enough for six donuts apiece, but I only want two, so you can have my other four," he told Chris.

Sticky, messy glazed donuts. The very worst. Chris grabbed a box and didn't stop eating them until they were all gone.

Miller's

by Cal Freeman

Cal is the author of the books Fight Songs *and* Poolside at the Dearborn Inn. *His writing has appeared in many journals including* The Oxford-American, Ninth Letter, Sugar House Review, The Poetry Review, *and* Hippocampus. *He is a recipient of the Devine Poetry Fellowship (judged by Terrance Hayes) and winner of Passages North's Neutrino Prize. He currently serves as music editor of* The Museum of Americana: A Literary Review *and teaches at Oakland University.*

Honor system, no bill left at your table. Cash only. Summarize what you had to the one who already knows when you are done. Plain burger medium, no cheese, two drafts, two whiskeys. Quick math and a total. I made it sound snappy when I had the energy. I'd repeat it in my head several times before I spoke. Plain burger medium no cheese two drafts two whiskeys.

Our snow day bar. Sleighs and horses and country inns and snowmen painted on the back mirror that winter night we stopped in to have burgers and Canadian Club and play a few games of euchre at a table in the corner. We could not see out, but we could sense it falling. To see is to sense, so maybe we didn't sense it, but we knew it was falling. Out there where we had just been with beards of slush in our knit hats.

When we left to walk home, the side door was stuck against a drift. I shouldered it like a sleigh and fell into the night. Behind the UPS store across the road, Molly found a hand truck a worker had forgotten to put away and proceeded to give Sarah and Emily rides between the staggered, windblown peaks of drifts. It gets beautiful and burdensome as it accumulates. We were warm from the food and whiskey, insulated from the wind and falling snow fine as eiderdown and heavy as a wet wool coat and we were ponderous as eider ducks walking through it. Molly left the hand truck where she found it. I'm sure there's some muddled footage of them cutting ruts in the alleyway and laughing.

The afternoons I spent there by myself were darker than that night. Same order. Here's to getting right. Fanny Howe's poems on the bar top next to my beer, a High Life draft with CC back. The same, always, burdensome and beautiful as you fall. Yet it wasn't the kind of place they'd shout your name or pretend to remember you. A High Life draft with CC back, plain burger no cheese with raw onion and pickle—you can feel human again if you repeat that order. High Life draft, CC back, plain burger, no cheese, raw onion and pickle. The Canadian Club would come in a big slug in a water glass, and they'd set the burger before you on a wax paper sheet.

The Early Bird in Winter
by Chris Dungey

Chris is a retired autoworker in Michigan. He hikes, rides mountain bikes, sings in a Presbyterian choir, and follows the Detroit City FC and Flint City Bucks FC with religious fervor. His collections The Pace-Lap Blues *and* We Won't Be Kissing *(in which this story is also included) can be found on Amazon/Kindle.*

There was Lynwood Bliss clearing the sidewalk in front of Thumb Edison, a goofy scarf wrapped over his tuque like a babushka. As always, his mouth hung open, wheezing a plume of vapor as he mumbled to himself. My gramps always told me that the early bird catches the worm. Today it looked like that bird would be Lynwood.

"Hullo, Lynwood. Hard at it?"

Maybe he didn't hear me. I propped my wide, aluminum shovel under the Christmas lights strung around the front window. I might as well go in and say hello to Gramps anyway, though Lynwood had beat me to the damn worm.

Gramps was behind the counter in a white shirt and string tie as always. I heard the crash of burnt-out light-bulbs customers had turned in as they dropped into a bin. Fresh ones in flimsy cardboard sleeves were already stacked and ready for exchange.

"Snow day, Heck boy? I must have left those piled on the hatch last' night."

I used to like pulling the lever to drop the bulbs when I was little.

"You like our new Christmas lights?"

"Yeah, I guess so. No dead ones yet. Hey, you gave Lynwood my job."

"Ol' egg-nuts? Yeah well, he's my right-hand man when you're not around. I can't have any slip-'n'-falls out there."

"I was surprised they called off school or I would've been here. It didn't seem like that much snow. So, I slept in a little."

"Yup, they missed on this one. Now the weatherman on Channel 12 says there's a lot more coming. You'll be getting new work all day. You wanna do the back walk for a buck?"

"Sure. I need some Christmas money. It's a lucky storm for me."

"Holidays are coming on fast, alright. I'm supposed to take your grandma shopping at the *Montgomery Ward* this weekend."

A jingle-bell above the door announced the entrance of Lynwood Bliss. He scuffed his big rubber boots on the mat, his thick glasses fogging over immediately.

I retrieved my shovel and carried it through the office to the back yard. Behind Thumb Edison, a narrow garden space extended to the alley. Gramps parked next to a row of trash burn barrels. Three-story buildings rose on either side of this little park. Between the *DeLuxe Theater* and the *Fox and Son's Mortuary*, Gramps' little alcove sat in perpetual shade. There were two apartments on the top floor of the little funeral parlor. I couldn't imagine sleeping through every bump-in-the-night from downstairs, but the tenants had a nice balcony space off the back.

Just out the door, I started removing a low drift with Gramps's galoshes prints tromped through it. I couldn't figure out how the wind managed to get back there. Maybe it was some kind of swirling effect caused by wind buffeting between the three walls and trying to get back out. *Cyclonic* was the word I must have picked up from Earth Science class. But the snow was light and fluffy so far. Easy to fling. Even wet snow never clung to my aluminum scooper. That baby held more than any domestic shovel I'd ever used. The snow stuck only to the mold-green cement where Gramps had stepped.

I cleared the walk all the way to the alley in no time. An easy dollar. I extended my work to make sure Gramps could get back into his Oldsmobile with dry feet, then a nice path around the burn barrels. When I shouldered the grain scoop and turned to go in, I nearly whopped Lynwood in the head.

"Whoa! Where'd *you* come from?"

"I didn't mean to startle ya."

"You snuck up on me."

"Loren said to spread the salt and I done it and then Loren said to burn the trash. I spread the salt out front, too."

Lynwood had dragged two cardboard boxes piled with refuse behind him. He pushed them up next to the first rusty barrel. Wadded up paper towel and Kleenex from the restroom; flimsy light-bulb cartons; all sorts of parts boxes. Thumb Edison still had a guy come into repair toasters and electric skillets in the basement workshop.

"You're a good man, Lynwood."

"I gotta burn this trash. It'll keep me warm."

"Well, good. I'll let you get on with it."

He had already turned to start hugging armloads of trash into the barrel. The whole lot of it might burn for ten minutes.

I crunched through the coarse salt toward the rear entrance of Thumb Edison. Lynwood had thrown it down so thickly that it looked like a smashed windshield on the concrete, like what the cops would sweep onto the shoulder after an accident. I paused at the back door to scrape my boots. The first whiff of smoke caught up to me, so I turned to see how Lynwood was doing.

The dirty grey smoke, drifting through a fresh white billow of snow, hid him from view for a moment. That vortex effect again, whirled the smoke around his scarf babushka. He began to cough, harsh and rasping, but didn't step away. Something crackled in the refuse, then burst like popcorn. Lynwood stayed right over the barrel, stirring the blaze with what looked like an old broomstick. Gasping, he finally turned his face aside. Maybe he'd brought out some solvent-soaked rags from the workshop, or plastic packing dividers. It smelled poisonous.

That's when I remembered Lynwood's special relationship to fire and smoke. He should have known better.

Every Monday evening at 7:30, the siren wailed from an antenna mast above Celeryville Fire Hall. You could set your watch by it. *Seven-thirty Monday night* folks told each other. The volunteers practiced their response times, cars hurtling down the village streets. They held a meeting, inspected their equipment then drank some beers. Gramps served as Assistant Chief. The citizen firemen let Lynwood hang around at the Hall. They handed him a push-broom when the pumper had been backed out from its bay to be washed and polished. He rode in all the parades like an acne-scarred Dalmatian mascot, sounding the klaxon in one long, painful blare until someone made him stop.

I didn't begrudge the guy these privileges. Well, maybe a little. He lived with an elderly mother and the story was that he'd been struck by a motorcycle as a little kid; knocked him ass-over-tea kettle. The head injury was severe, and he was never right after that. He had the intelligence of a third-grader folks said. Where anyone could have learned *this* detail, I don't know. But I supposed he could read on some level. It had once pissed me off that he'd gotten the very last fireman's hat. Even Gramps couldn't save me one. It was my own fault, and I was equally mad at myself, so I forgot about it. I didn't think the fire department was doing him any favor though, letting him wear that goofy thing around until the weather got cold.

Yeah, okay. That had been another early-bird reminder. Again, I was the late one. To celebrate Michigan Fire Prevention week, the Celeryville volunteers had passed out red, plastic, replica helmets with a gold *CFD* sticker on the front. We had already sat through the stop-drop-and-roll, crawl-near-the-floor assembly at school. The Chief, Reverend Corbit, a local Methodist minister and war hero, had invited everyone up through 7th grade to come for a demonstration of the big hydraulic ladder down at the Fire Hall after school. I must have gotten distracted somewhere along the few blocks to downtown. I picked up the pace just in time to see Gramps hand Lynwood the last helmet. Saving it for me wouldn't have been fair and maybe he thought I had outgrown such a silly, little kid's toy.

The white smoke parted momentarily. I saw Lynwood slip to one knee. Now he was retching, deep and sustained. I ran back to the barrel. With his stick, he had fished out a melting tangle of green wiring and charred Christmas bulbs. He still clung to the stick, now propped over the lip of the fire. The bulbs smoldered like a ruined bag of marshmallows. *Well, no s'mores for this Cub Scout.* I took the stick from his gloved hand. The glob of wiring hung by a few gooey, stretching filaments then dropped back into the flames.

"What happened, Lynwood? You shouldn't breathe that stuff."

He crawled a few feet away from the barrel. I put my hand on his shoulder, ready to help him stand.

"Them musta fell in by accident, Heck boy. I didn't put 'em in on purpose. I did'n' even see 'em."

"No, no. Of course not."

He rose unsteadily to his feet.

"Loren, though. I don't know what *he'll* say. He might not like it so good."

To my mind, that could have happened quite easily. The repair bench in the basement was a clutter of wire bits, solder splatters, and small tools. I brushed off Lynwood's coat. He brushed the packed snow and slush from his wet corduroy knees.

"Gramps won't care, as long as you're OK. You better come away from there now. Get some fresh air in your lungs."

He made a display, then, of gasping in great draughts of the blustering wind. He began coughing again but was giggling, too.

"Hector boy, I musta swallowed…I just swallowed some snowflakes."

"You swallowed some nasty chemical smoke is what. Snowflakes won't hurt you."

"Them wires musta just fell in the box, I'll tell Loren. It was by accident. I gotta get my shovel."

Lynwood walked slowly toward the rear entrance to Thumb Edison. A new squall of snow whipped in so thickly that I could hardly see him. When he was done telling his story to Gramps, I figured he'd head down Almont Street again, getting the jump on me. Girard's Barber Shop and the Western Auto Store would need shoveling, and then on around the corner to McBride's Meat Locker and Jewel Pharmacy, all of them a renewable goldmine today for ambitious kids of all ages.

Equally disturbing to me as I tidied up around Gramps's Oldsmobile, was a sudden realization that I might have had to perform that new breath-of-life technique on Lynwood. Knowing how to do it was included in getting the First Aid badge in Scouts. I had only done it effectively twice on that dummy, Respiration Rhonda. You had to blow your brains out just to get her chest to move. Then we wiped her lips off with an antiseptic swab for the next guy. Could I put my mouth right on ol' Lynwood and start breathing for him? If you made the mistake of staring, it looked like he almost never brushed his teeth. I guess I could have done it. At that point, he wouldn't be competing for my work at least.

I shouldered my grain scoop again. The flames were gone from the tight, flaking wad of paper ash in the barrel. The knot of fused wiring sat in the middle of the last embers, still giving off a chemical stink. I trudge down the alley toward 4th Street. I would collect my dollar later when I cleaned up this job again in the afternoon. My hope now was that Gramps would tell Lynwood he ought to just go on home. As a designated right-hand man, he'd have to listen to Gramps.

www.ingramcontent.com/pod-product-compliance
Lightning Source LLC
Chambersburg PA
CBHW070359200726
48294CB00003B/999